THE HATEFUL HORRORS OF THE
QUEEN OF HEARTS

STEVE BARLOW - STEVE SKIDMORE
ILLUSTRATED BY PIPI SPOSITO

Franklin Watts
First published in Great Britain in 2020
by The Watts Publishing Group

Text © Steve Barlow and Steve Skidmore 2020
Illustrations © Franklin Watts 2020
Design: Cathryn Gilbert

The authors and illustrator have asserted their rights in
accordance with the Copyright, Designs and Patents Act, 1988.

ISBN 978 1 4451 7015 2
ebook ISBN 978 1 4451 7017 6
Library ebook ISBN 978 1 4451 7016 9

1 3 5 7 9 10 8 6 4 2

Printed in Great Britain

MIX
Paper from
responsible sources
FSC
www.fsc.org
FSC® C104740

Franklin Watts
An imprint of
Hachette Children's Group
Part of The Watts Publishing Group
Carmelite House
50 Victoria Embankment
London EC4Y 0DZ

An Hachette UK Company
www.hachette.co.uk

www.franklinwatts.co.uk

HOW TO BE A MEGAHERO

Some superheroes can read books with their X-ray vision without opening the covers or even when they're in a different room ...

Others can read them while flying through the air or stopping a runaway train.

But that stuff *IS* just small potatoes to you, because you're not a superhero. You're a *MEGAHERO*!

YES, this book is about **YOU**! And you don't just read it to the end and then stop. You read a bit: then you make a choice that takes you to a different part of the book. You might jump from Section 3 to 47 or 28!

If you make a good choice, *GREAT!*

BUUUUUUT ...

If you make the wrong choice ... *DA-DA-DAAAH!*

ALL KINDS OF BAD STUFF WILL HAPPEN.

Too bad! It's no good turning green and tearing your shirt off. You'll just have to start again. But that won't happen, will it?

Because you're not a zero, or even a superhero. You are ... *MEGAHERO*!

You are a **BRILLIANT INVENTOR** — but one day **THE SUPER PARTICLE-ACCELERATING COSMIC RAY COLLIDER** you'd made out of old drinks cans, lawnmower parts and a mini black hole went critical and scrambled your molecules (nasty!). When you finally stopped screaming, smoking and bouncing off the walls, you found your body had changed! Now you can transform into any person, creature or object. HOW AWESOME IS THAT?*!!!*

You communicate with your **MEGACOMPUTER** companion, **PAL**, through your **MEGASHADES** sunglasses (which make you look pretty COOL, too). **PAL** controls the things you turn into and *almost hardly ever crashes and has to be turned off and on again!* This works perfectly — unless you have a bad WIFI signal, or **PAL** gets something wrong — but hey! That's computers for you, right?

Like all heroes, your job is to SAVE THE WORLD from **BADDIES AND THEIR EVIL SCHEMES**. But be back in time for supper. Even **MEGAHEROES** have to eat ...

Go to 1.

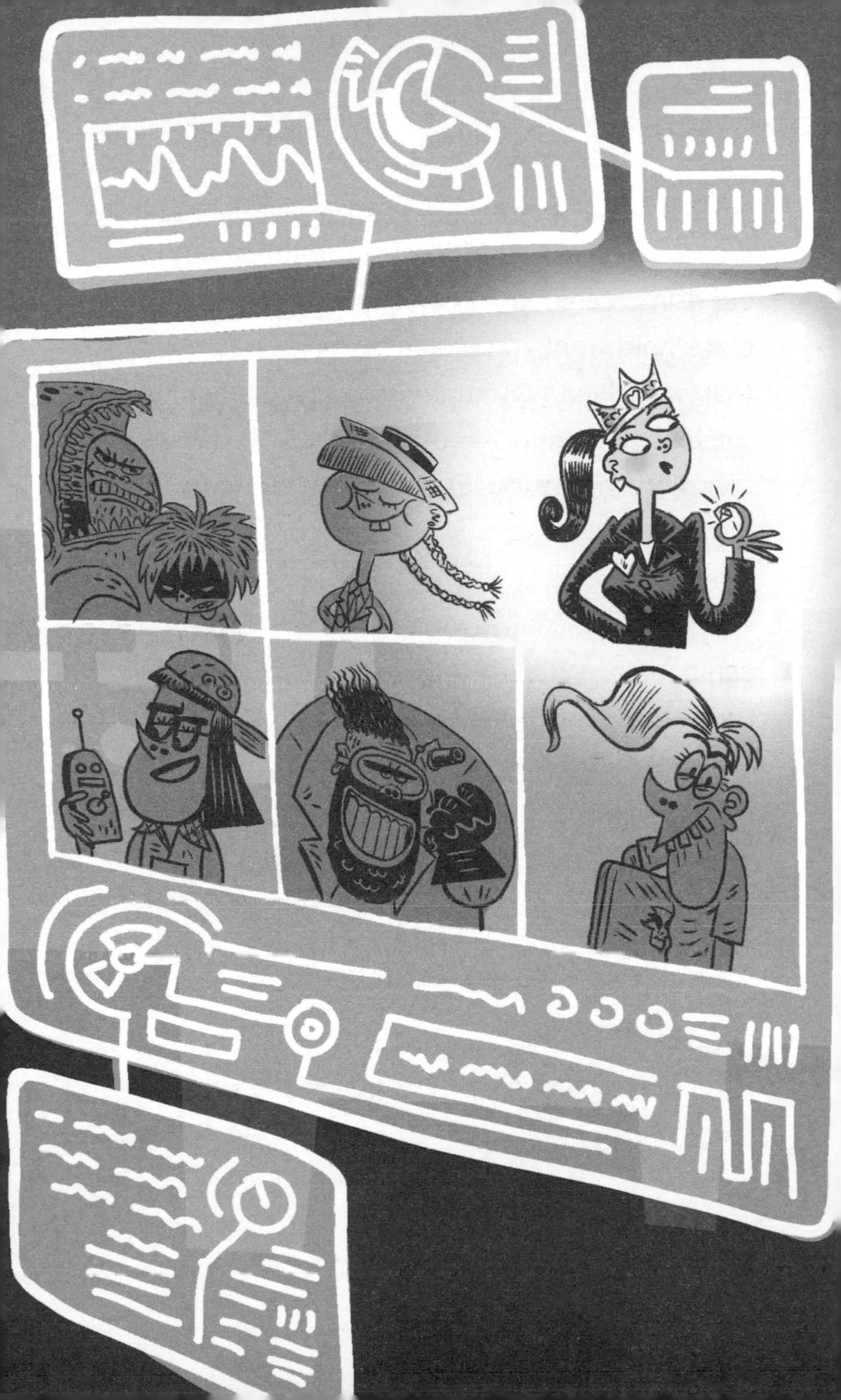

1

You are in the **MEGA** cave playing a game of cards with PAL.

You lay down the KING OF SPADES.

"**SNAP!**" says PAL.

"But you haven't even played your card yet!" you protest.

The KING OF SPADES appears on PAL's holographic screen.

"How did you know?" you ask.

"I CAN PREDICT WHAT'S COMING NEXT," says PAL, smugly.

Suddenly the **MEGA ALARM** rings out.

"**CRIME ALERT! CRIME ALERT!**"

"You didn't predict that," you say.

"IT'S PROBABLY NOT IMPORTANT!" replies PAL.

To see what the crime is, go to 24.
To carry on playing cards, go to 48.

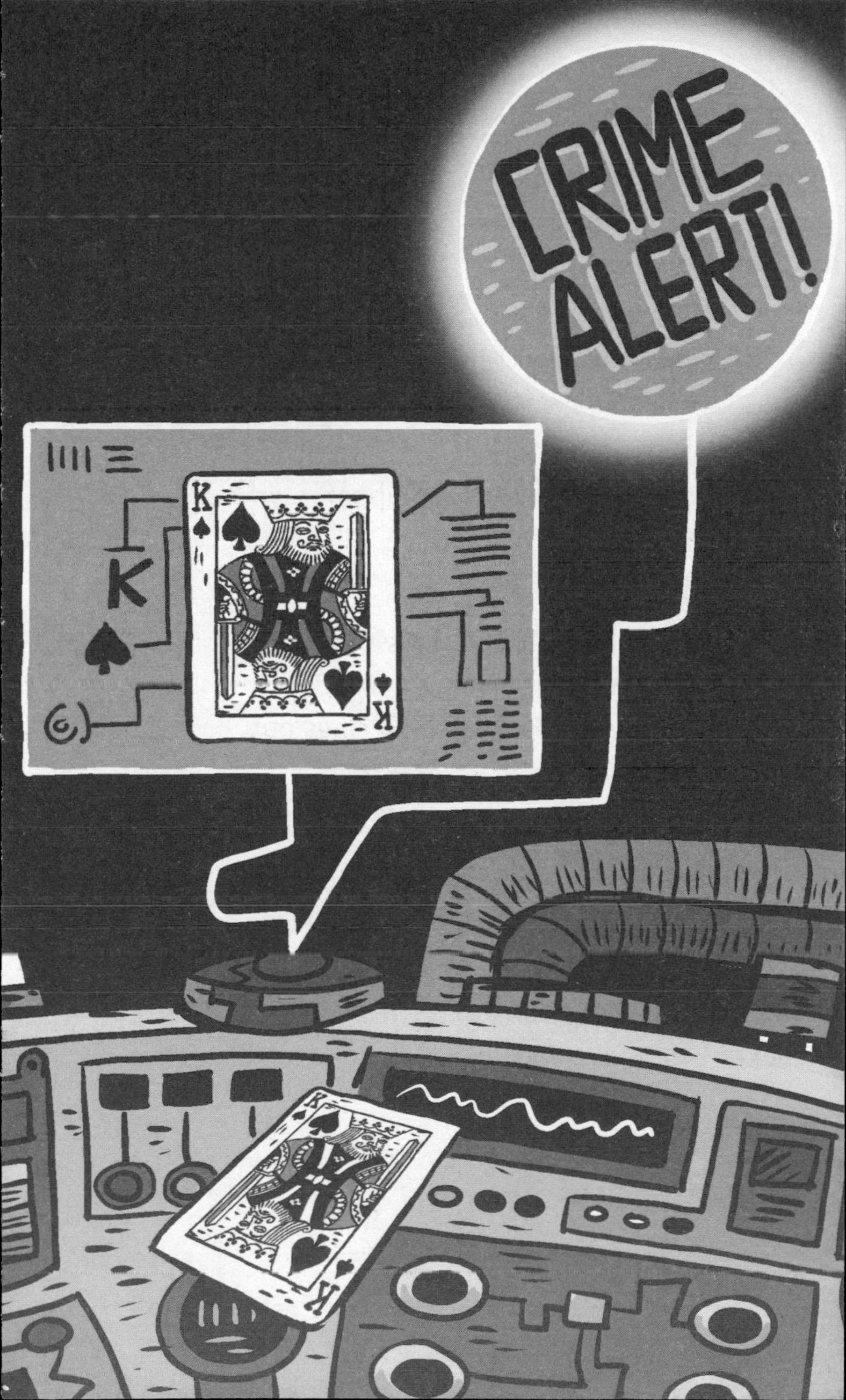
CRIME ALERT!

2

You transform into human form. "So, **Clubs**, you're after the Crown jewels. Where are the guards?"

"**HUR, HUR,**" **Clubs** laughs. "The queen sorted them out."

"And where is she now?"

"In the jewel room," replies **Clubs**, "with **Spades** and **Diamonds**. You're too late, **MEGAHERO**. I'm going to deal with you ..." Raising a clubbed hand, he steps forward.

To turn into an axe, go to 21.

To turn into a flame, go to 13.

3

"What's next on your **CRIMES TO-DO LIST**, Your Majesty?" you hear **Diamonds** ask.

"We're going to commit the biggest diamond robbery *ever*!" answers the queen.

As you move forward to hear more clearly, your tail brushes against the wall. A piece of rock is dislodged and falls.

The queen spots you. "Hello, foxy, or rather, **MEGAHERO**! I thought you'd follow us. Have a welcome card."

She throws a playing card towards you. It explodes, bringing the tunnel crashing down.

To head towards the gang, go to 42.

To head back out of the tunnel, go to 49.

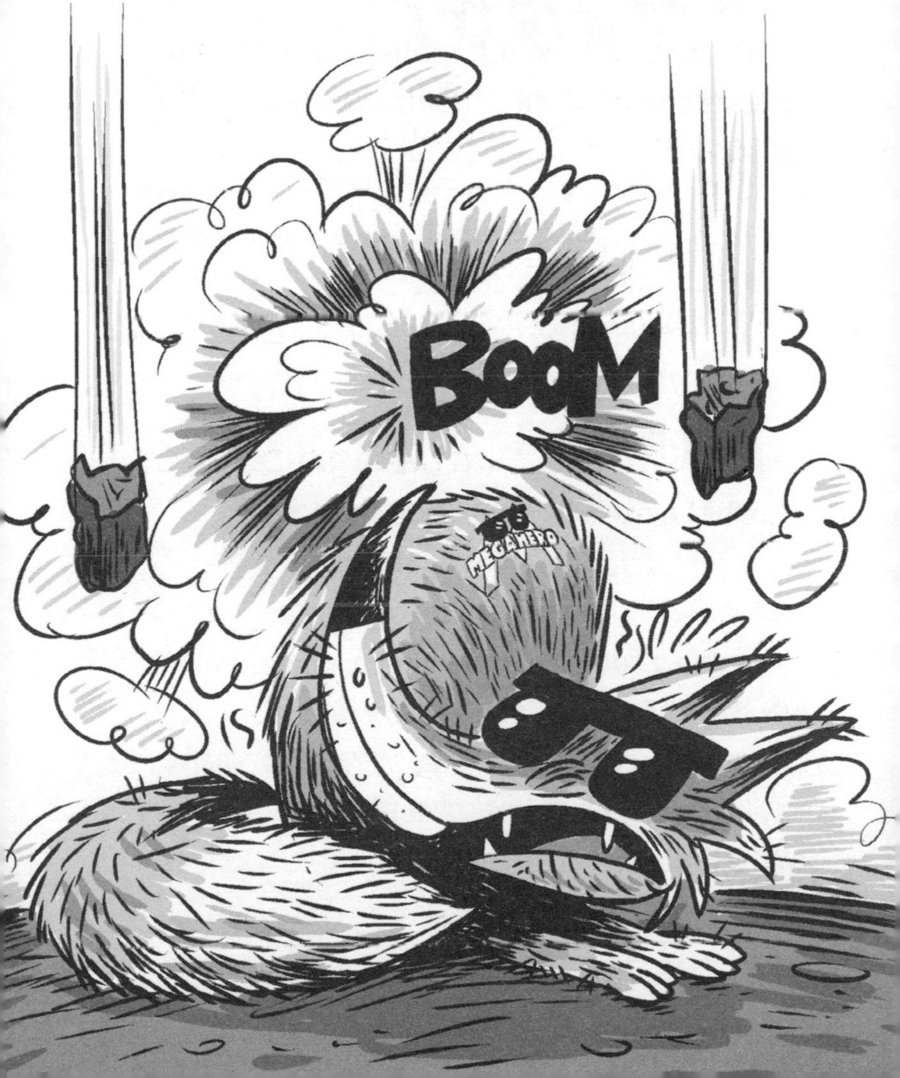
BOOM
MEGAHERO

You turn back into human form and head into the steel vault. It contains several large canisters, but the diamonds have gone.

Suddenly ...

The steel door shuts behind you and knockout gas pours out of the canisters.

"PAL, turn me into a gas mask!" you cry. But there is no reply. The steel walls are too thick and you can't make contact.

You are helpless as the knockout gas fills the airtight vault.

DA-DA-DAAAH!

What a GAS-tly blunder! *Go back to 1.*

"I'm going to head to the Tower immediately!" you say. "Turn me into a tourist!"

"THAT'S A CRAZY IDEA," says PAL. "YOU WON'T GET INTO THE TOWER NOW, IT'S LOCKED UP AT NIGHT."

You realise PAL is right.

Go to 19.

6

You move towards the door as fast as your legs can carry you. Unfortunately, despite having hundreds of legs, you don't move very quickly! The raven's sharp beak spears towards you.

DA-DA-DAAAH!

That bird was RAVEN-ous! *Go back to 1.*

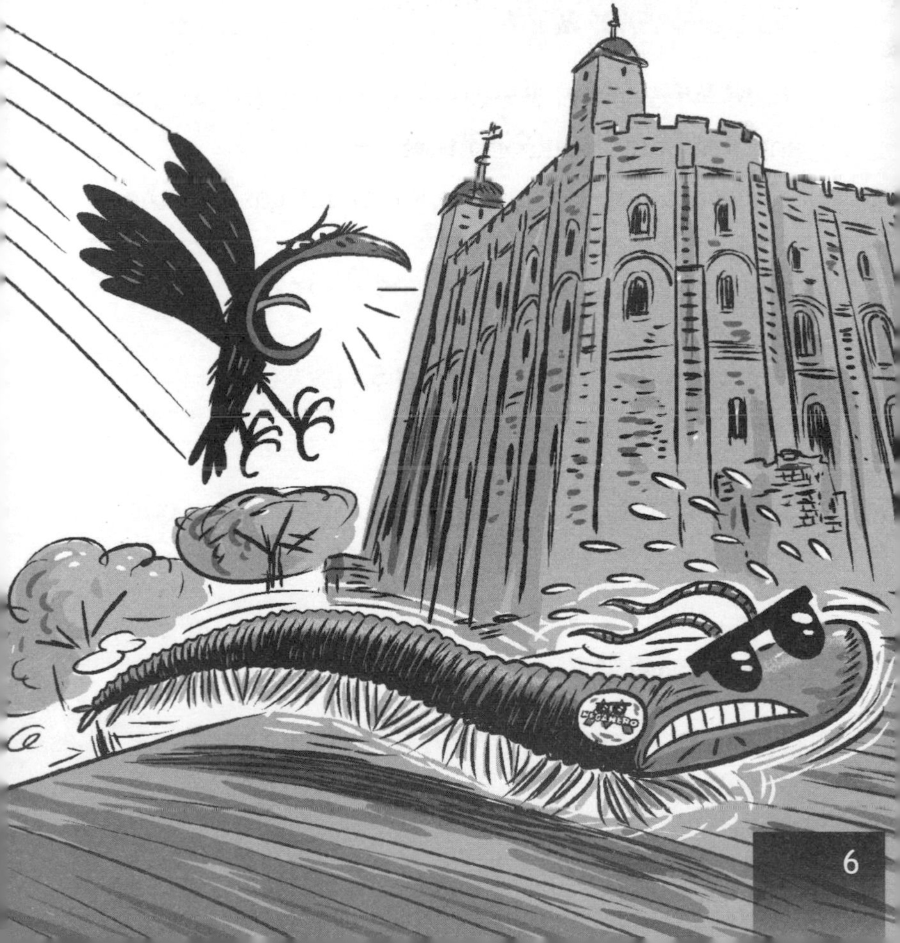

7

"I'm coming to Antwerp right now." You pause. "*Er ... where is it?*"

"In Belgium," replies the director.

"Great! *Er ...* where's Belgium?" you ask.

"In Europe," she sighs.

You are **EMBARRASSED**. "OK, so I don't know *EVERYTHING*. I'm a *MEGAHERO* not a *GEOGRAPHY HERO*. I'll be with you very soon!"

To turn into a stealth jet, go to 30.
To turn into a rocket, go to 16.

8

You switch to drone form and fly towards the Jewel Tower.

Suddenly ...

You are hit by a taser missile that takes out your electrics and your **COMMS**. You plummet earthwards.

DA-DA-DAAAH!

You're about to have a smashing time!
Go back to 1.

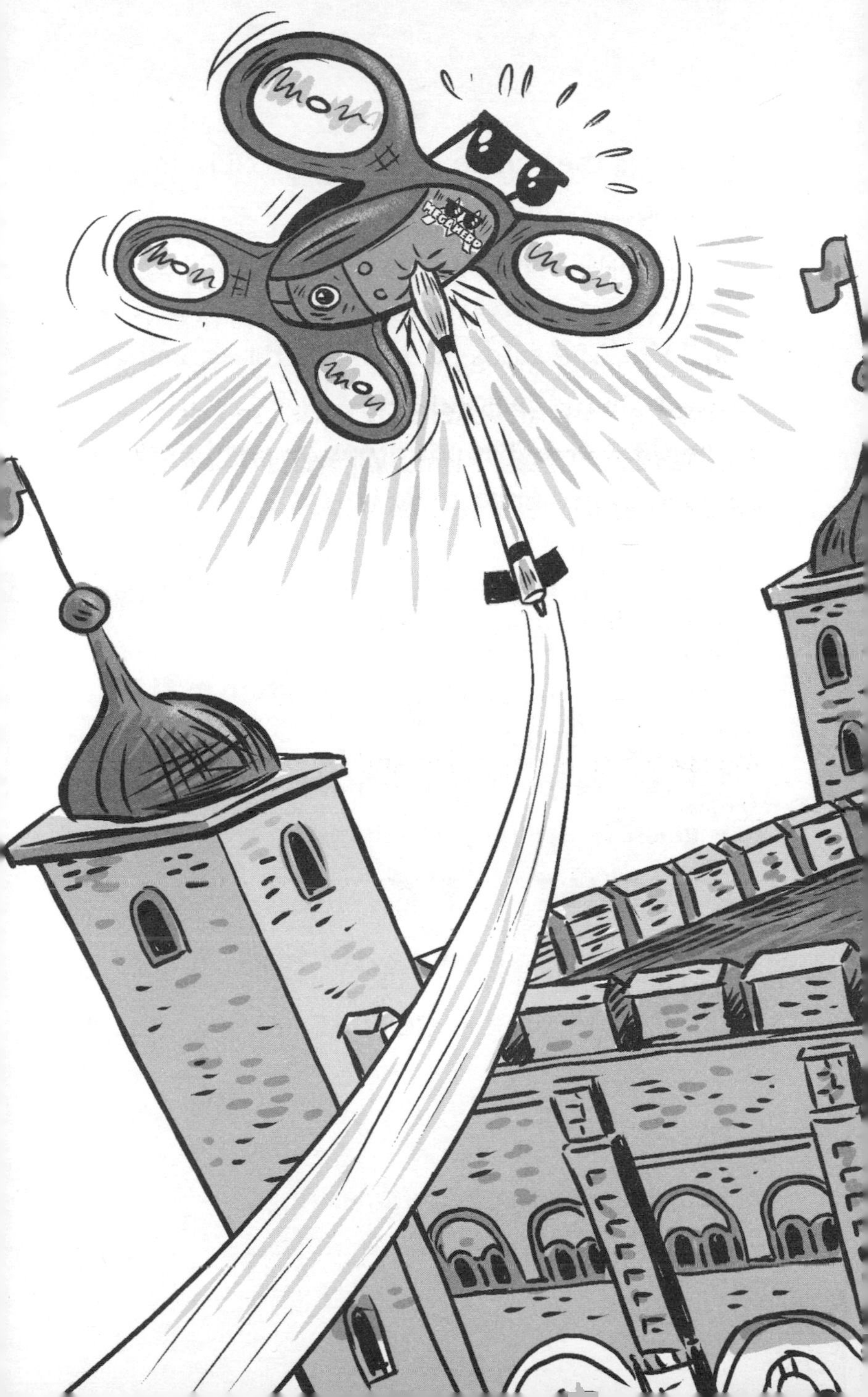
MEGA HERO

You fly into the middle of the gang. "Turn me into a metal cage," you tell PAL.

You transform into a cage, trapping the gang.

"Hello, *MEGAHERO*," says the QUEEN OF HEARTS. "The cards told me you'd be coming! Deal with him, Diamonds!"

The Jack of Diamonds drops his bag to reveal diamond-tipped fingers. He begins to cut through your metal bars.

"Did you know that diamonds can cut through metal?" laughs the queen.

"*OW!* I do now," you reply. "PAL, turn me into something else, quickly!"

But you are too late, Diamonds cuts through your glasses, leaving you helpless.

DA-DA-DAAAH!

Diamonds are not your best friend!
Go back to 1.

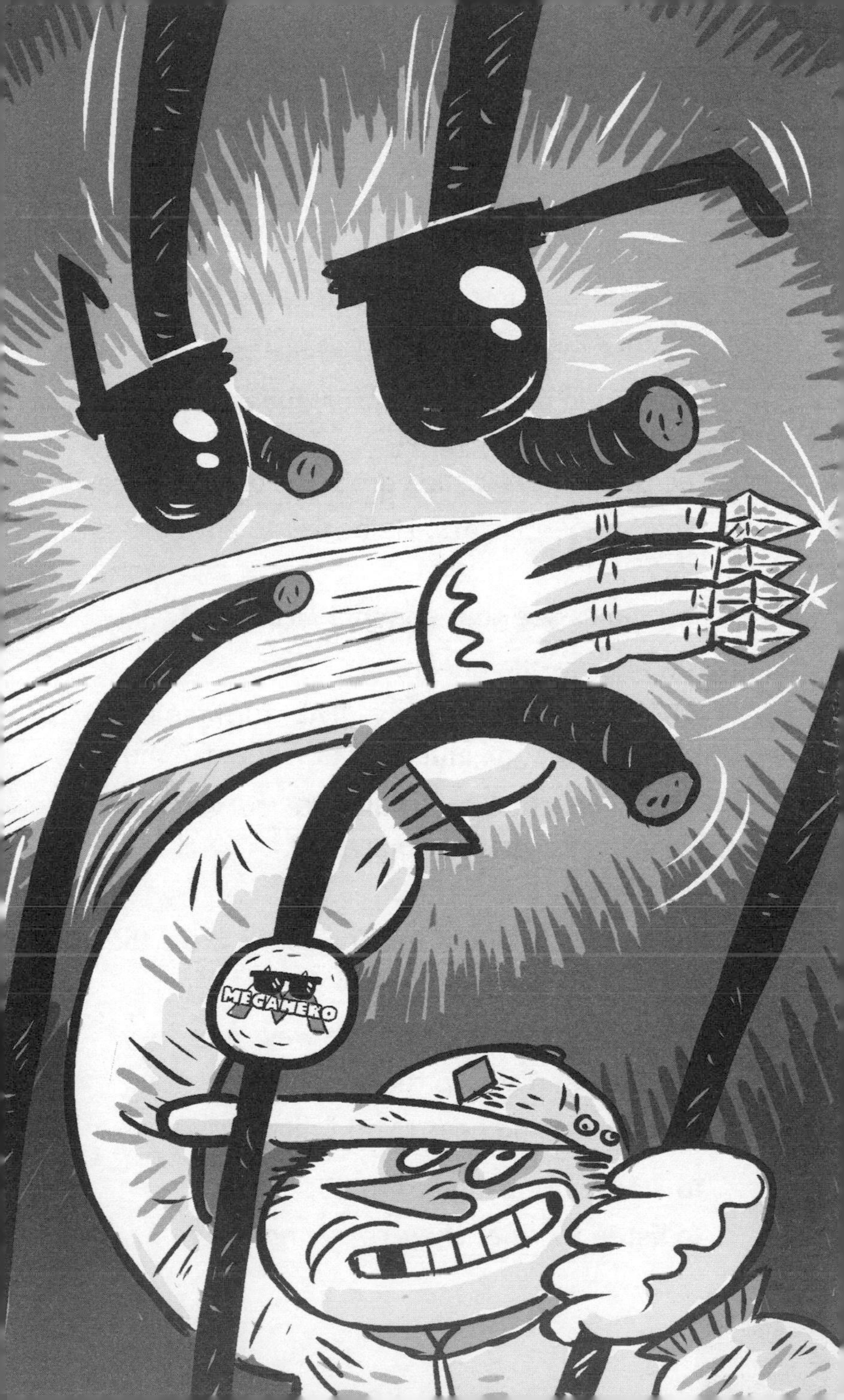
MEGAHERO

10

She throws a playing card at you. It hits you in the face and sticks to your eyes!

Blinded, you try to grab hold of the card, but your spade-like hands can't remove it!

"Stuck and bust!" laughs the queen. Before you can contact PAL for help, you feel a crack to the head and drop to the floor, unconscious.

DA-DA-DAAAH!

You didn't see that coming! *Go back to 1.*

11

"Turn me into a fox and I'll follow them." You suddenly can't move. "I said **FOX**, not a **BOX**!"

"SORRY, THE **COMMS** ARE TERRIBLE."

"So are you!"

You transform into a fox and speed after the gang.

The tunnel goes on for some way. Your foxy sense of smell picks up the gang's scent. You creep forward and hear them talking.

To attack the gang, go to 25.
To listen to what they're saying, go to 3.

"I'll stay as a jet," you say. "Direct me to DIAMOND HEADQUARTERS."

Thirty minutes later, you zoom into land in Antwerp's diamond district. There are dozens of police officers surrounding DIAMOND HQ.

You turn back into human form.

The officers are amazed. "Wow, _MEGAHERO_! We didn't see or hear you until you were right overhead!"

You smile. "That was the plan. Where's the gang?"

"Still inside the building," explains an officer. "When they come out, we'll grab them."

To head inside the building, go to 27.

To wait for the gang to come out, go to 34.

"Light me up, PAL," you say.

As Clubs brings down his hand, you turn into a roaring flame.

The villain's hand catches fire. "**OW!** Dat hurts!" Clubs hops about as the flame spreads to his other hand. "Put it out!"

"Certainly." You turn into a high-pressure hosepipe and shoot a torrent of water. Clubs slams against a stone wall and drops to the floor.

"The fire's out. And so's he," you laugh. "Now get me into the Jewel Tower, PAL, I've got a robbery to stop!"

Go to 31.

14

Your pride is stung. You become human and glare at the queen. "How did you know I was here?"

"My cards said you would be."

"What does she mean, PAL?" you whisper.

"SHE'S USING THE CARDS TO WORK OUT WHAT WILL HAPPEN NEXT," replies PAL. "A BIT LIKE MY PREDICTING ABILITY!"

The queen flings her hands forward and suddenly the air is filled with playing cards streaming like missiles towards you.

To attack the queen, go to 44.

To defend yourself, go to 36.

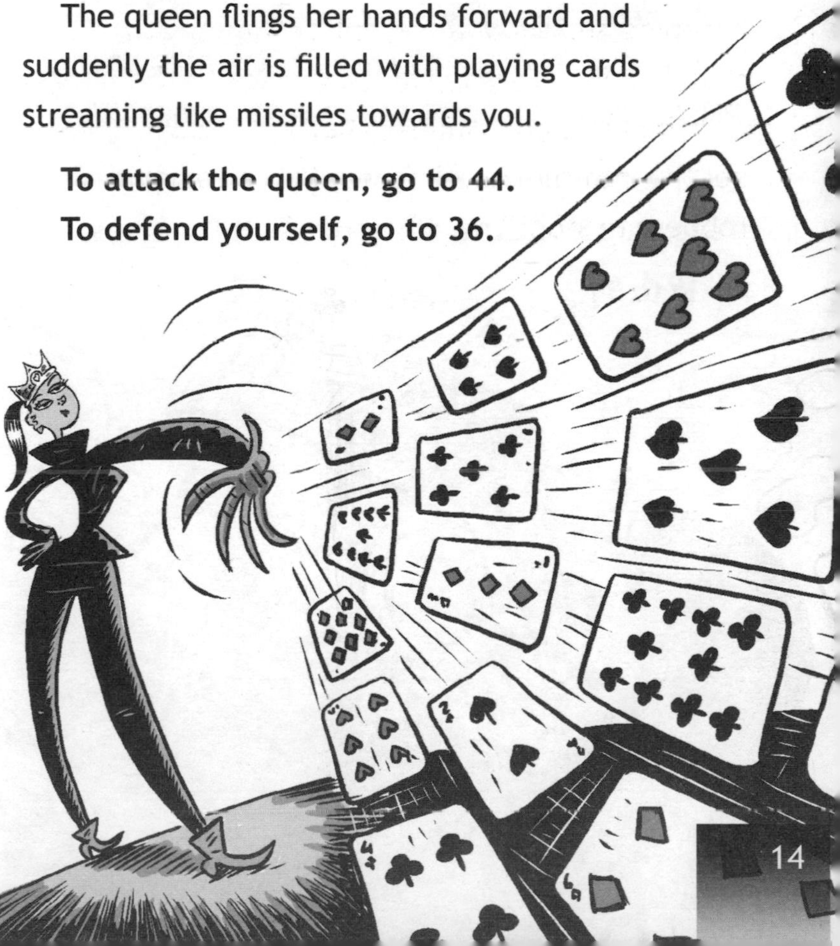

15

"Turn me into a bulldozer," you say.

Suddenly you grow horns, let out a bellow and feel very, very tired.

"I said a **BULLDOZER**, not a **DOZY BULL**!"

PAL corrects the mistake and you speed through the tunnel, pushing earth aside. Finally you burst into DIAMOND HQ.

"Where's the gang?" you ask PAL.

"THEY'VE DISAPPEARED. I CAN'T TRACE THEM AT ALL," PAL tells you. "WHAT DO YOU WANT TO DO NOW?"

To examine the evidence you have, go to 39.

To check out the diamond vault for clues, go to 4.

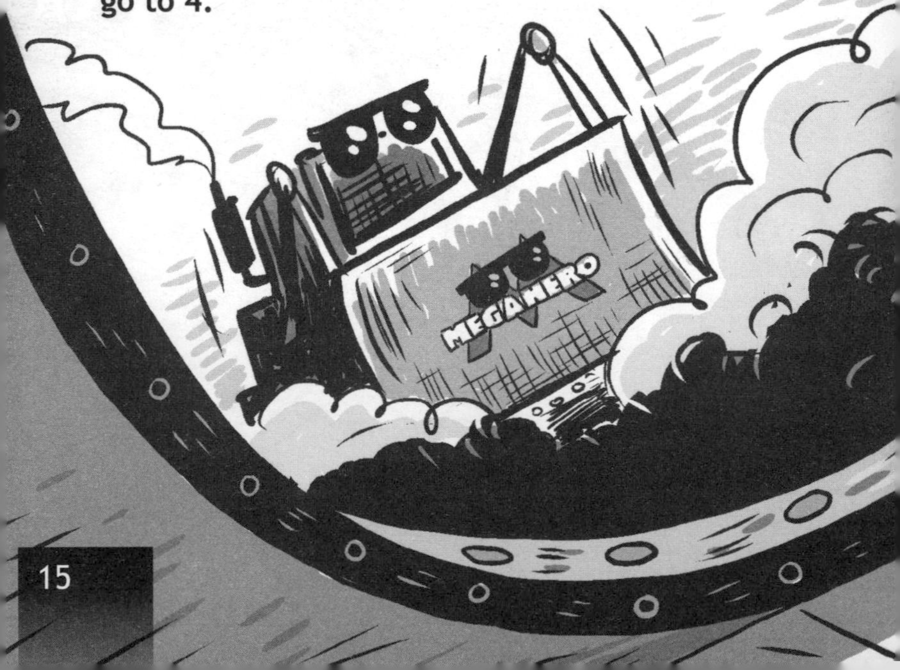
MEGAHERO

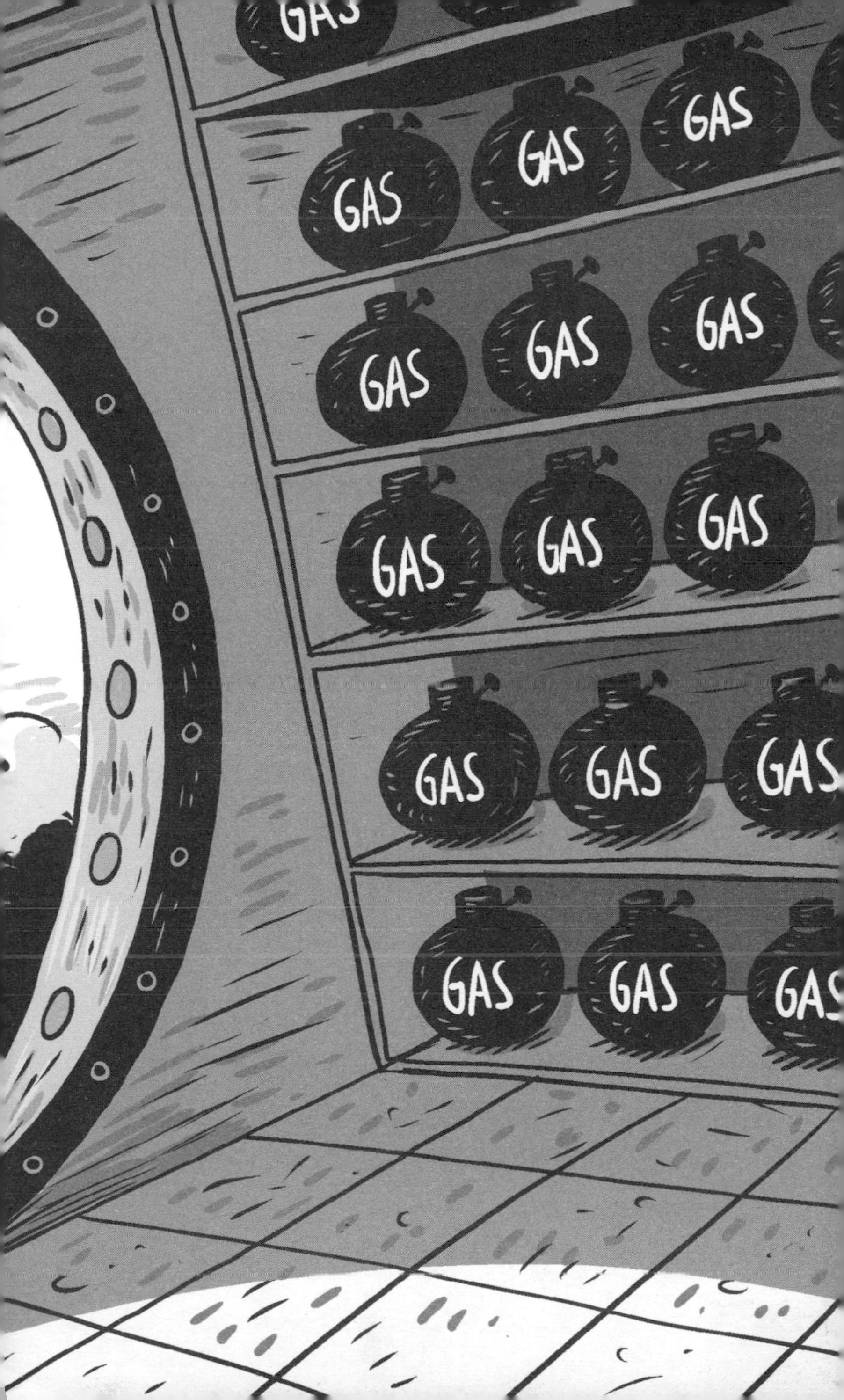
GAS
GAS
GAS
GAS
GAS
GAS
GAS
GAS
GAS
GAS
GAS
GAS
GAS
GAS

16

"Turn me into a rocket," you tell PAL.

Suddenly you are playing a guitar and singing loudly into a microphone. "*Baybeeeh, I love yooooou!*"

"THAT'S VERY KIND OF YOU TO SAY SO," replies PAL.

"I said a **ROCKET**, not a **ROCK STAR!**"

"**OOPS**," says PAL. "SORRY. BUT I DON'T THINK A ROCKET IS A GOOD IDEA. THE GANG WILL HEAR YOU COMING AND HOW WILL YOU LAND?"

"I can get there and then change into something else," you reply.

"AT THAT SPEED? I PREDICT THAT WON'T WORK!"

If you think PAL is right, go to 30.

If you insist on being a rocket, go to 43.

17

You leap towards Diamonds. "Fooled you!" you cry. "I'm not Spades, I'm really *MEGAHERO*!"

The queen laughs. "I knew that. The cards told me what you'd do. And now, I'm going to deal with you!"

Go to 10.

18

You turn into a wasp and zoom downstairs.

Suddenly PAL gives you a warning, "**VILLAINS DETECTED!**"

You fly around the corner to see the **QUEEN OF HEARTS** and her gang emerging from the diamond vault. She holds a pack of playing cards in her hand.

To follow the gang, go to 46.

To try and capture them, go to 9.

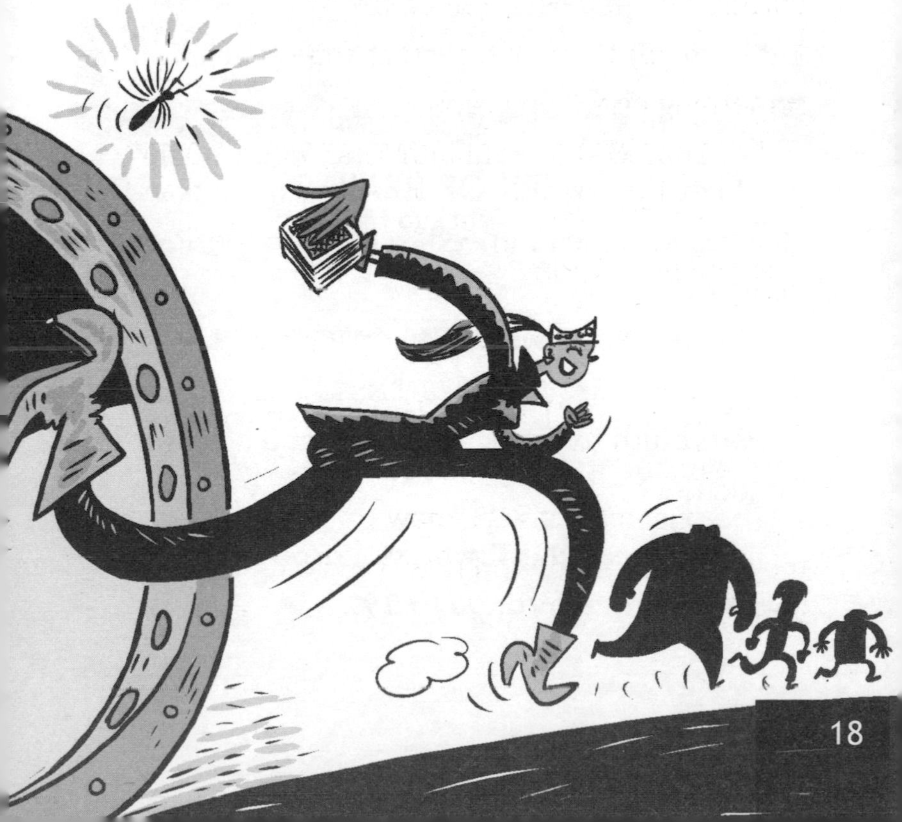

19

"Tell me about the Crown jewels," you say.

"THE CROWN AND SCEPTRE CONTAIN THE TWO LARGEST CUT DIAMONDS IN THE WORLD. THERE ARE OVER 23,000 DIAMONDS AND PRECIOUS GEMSTONES IN THE COLLECTION. THEY ARE KEPT IN A BULLETPROOF GLASS CASE IN THE JEWEL HOUSE AND GUARDED BY ARMED SOLDIERS."

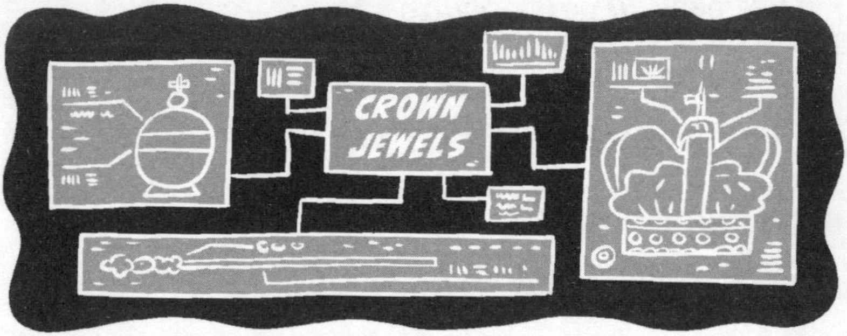
CROWN
JEWELS

"I bet the **QUEEN OF HEARTS** has a plan for dealing with them. I need to get into the Tower tonight."

"BE CAREFUL," warns PAL, "THE TOWER HAS SOME HI-TECH SECURITY SYSTEMS IN PLACE."

You return to jet-fighter form, and head for London.

To approach the Tower as a drone, go to 8.

To fly in as a bird, go to 29.

20

Realising the diamonds have gone, you turn back into human form and explore the building; but there is no sign of the gang.

Crystal Gems appears. She is furious. "You've taken too long! The gang have gone and so have the diamonds. We don't need you any more."

A *MEGAHERO* gets on with the job!
Go back to 1.

21

"Turn me into an axe," you tell PAL.

You turn into a packet of crisps. "Not a snack!" you cry.

"Yum, yum," says Clubs. "Snack attack!" Before you can transform again, his clubbed hands crash down on you, crunching you to smithereens.

CRUMBS! Go back to 1.

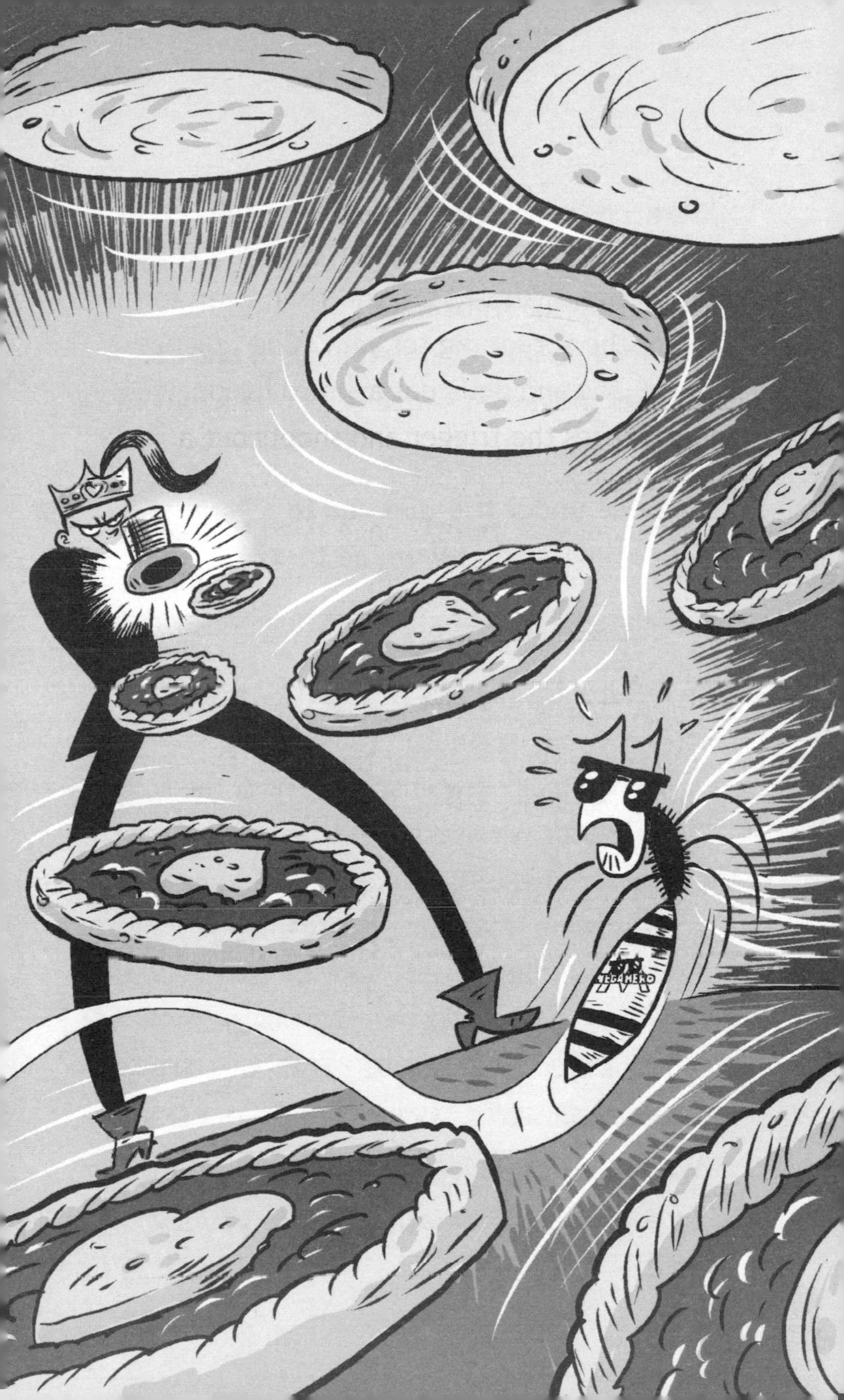

"I won't be stung by your insults!" you say.

"Stung? Nice clue." The queen looks at her cards. "The cards tell me you're in wasp form! I've got the very thing for you." She reaches into her bag and pulls out a weird looking gun. She squeezes the trigger and shoots out a **JAM TART!**

"The **Jack of Hearts** once tried to steal these from me — he doesn't work for me any more!" She pulls the trigger again, sending out a stream of tarts.

"**JAM! MMMMM!**" Your wasp instincts attract you to the jammy scent of the tarts. One hits, trapping you in its sticky sweetness, and you drop to the floor.

"PAL, get me out of here!" you cry. But the jam has blocked up your **COMMS**. The queen stands over you, foot raised ...

DA-DA-DAAAH!

You've come to a sticky end! *Go back to 1.*

23

You transform into a millipede.

But before you can scuttle under the door, a dark figure looms over you.

You look up into the open beak of one of the Tower of London's ravens. You're about to become a midnight snack!

To head under the door, go to 6.

To deal with the raven, go to 37.

24

"I'm *MEGAHERO*, my job is to STOP crime, no matter how big or small!" you say.

A worried looking woman pops onto the screen.

"*MEGAHERO*! We need you! I'm Crystal Gems, the Director of the Diamond District in Antwerp. A criminal gang is stealing our diamonds. Help!"

"ANTWERP IS THE LARGEST DIAMOND CENTRE IN THE WORLD," says PAL. "OVER 54 BILLION DOLLARS OF DIAMONDS ARE SOLD THERE EVERY YEAR. THIS SOUNDS LIKE A **MEGA** CRIME!"

To head to Antwerp IMMEDIATELY, go to 7.

To get more information before you set off, go to 38.

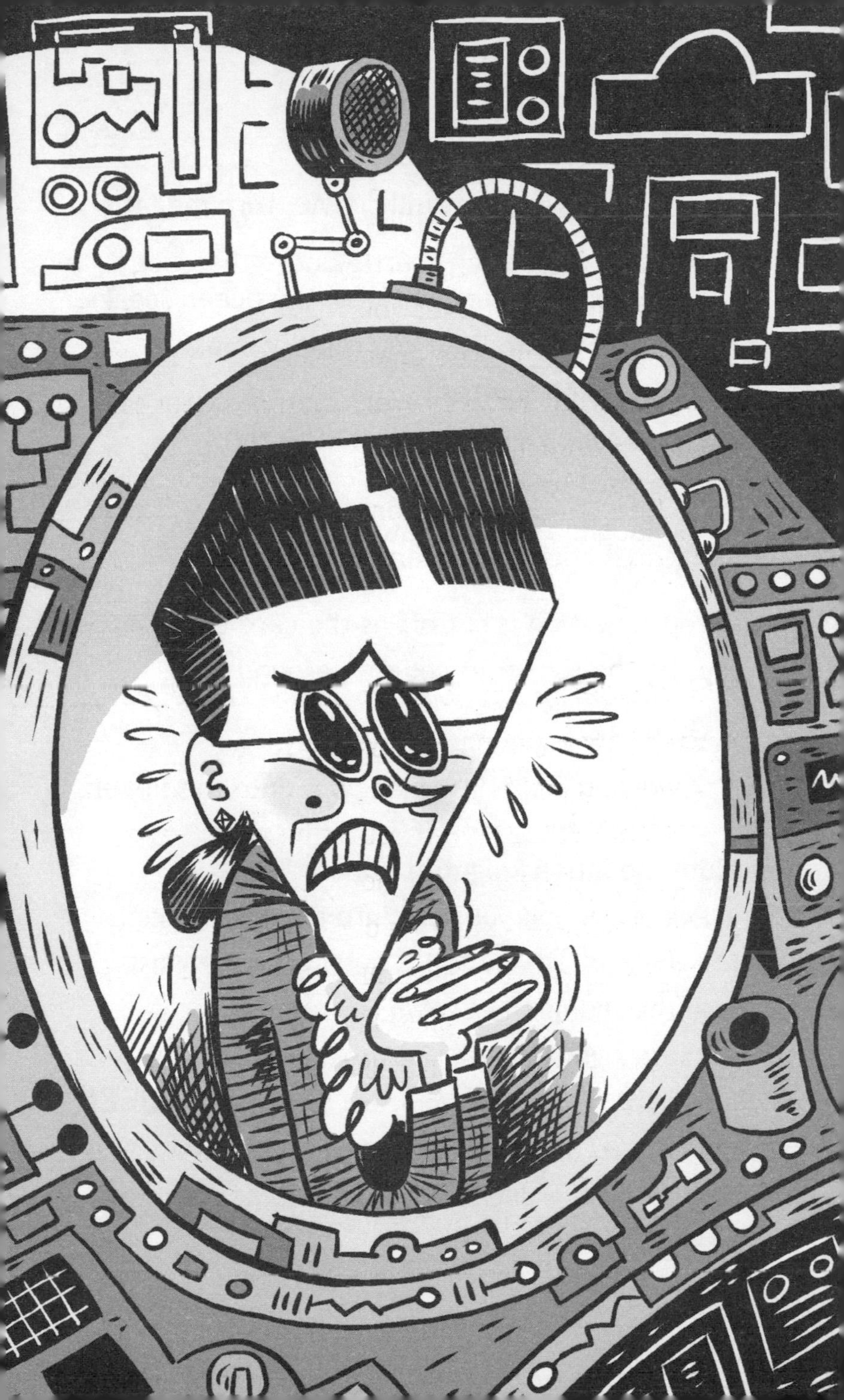

25

You move forward carefully. "PAL, turn me into a—"

But before you can continue, the queen speaks. "Hello, **MEGAHERO**. Glad you could join us!"

You've been spotted!

"Here's my welcome card!" She throws a playing card towards you.

You laugh. "What's that little thing going to ...?"

Your question is cut off as the card explodes, causing the tunnel to collapse around you!

Go to 42.

26

"Turn me into a knight in armour."

PAL obeys and you rush into the jewel room. The Jack of Diamonds is cutting at the glass case that holds the Crown jewels.

"Stop right there!" you order.

"I don't think so!" You turn to see the QUEEN OF HEARTS holding a can of pepper spray. "I get this from a duchess friend of mine. Her cook makes it."

She points it at your visor and presses the nozzle.

"**OWWWW!**" Your eyes feel as though they are on fire and you drop to the floor.

The queen sprays you again. "Diamonds, show ***MEGAHERO*** how your fingers can cut through anything, even metal armour!"

Diamonds moves towards you, fingers glistening.

DA-DA-DAAAH!

Goodnight, good knight! *Go back to 1.*

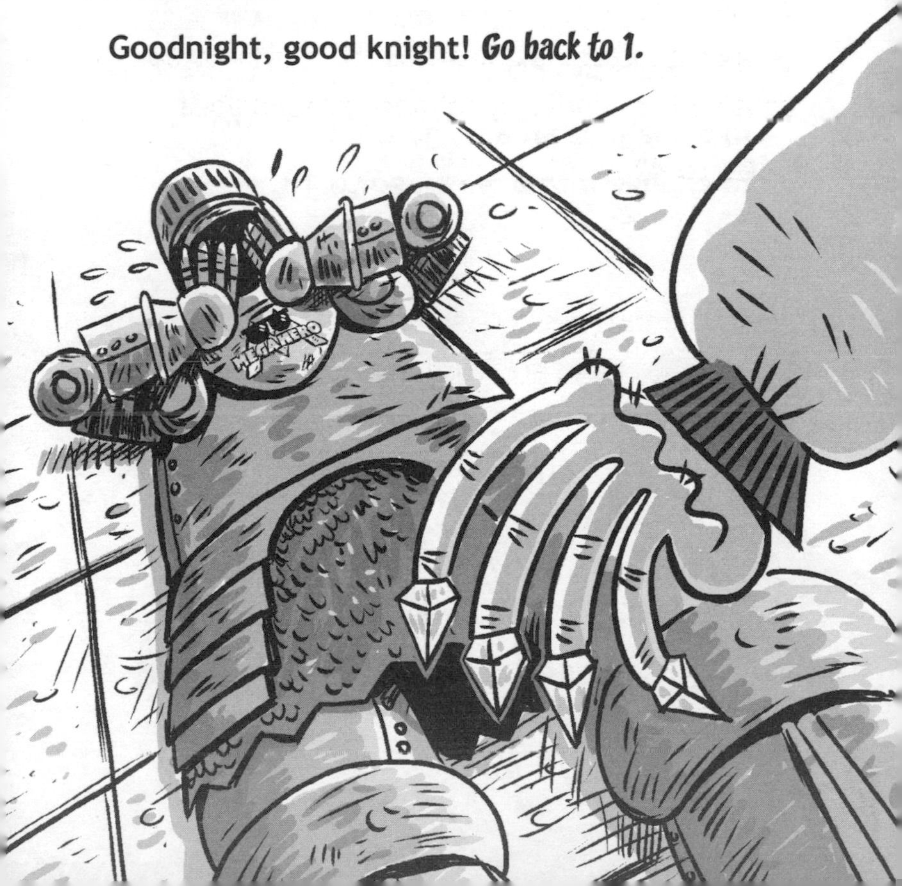
MEGAHERO

"Turn me into an ant," you tell PAL, "so I can sneak in."

PAL obeys and you scurry into the building, unnoticed. You see several guards lying on the floor, unconscious.

"There's a smell of gas," you tell PAL. "Maybe the gang used it to knock out the guards. But where are they now?"

"I'M DETECTING NOISE COMING FROM DOWNSTAIRS, IN THE VAULT AREA," says PAL.

To remain as an ant, go to 40.
To change into a wasp, go to 18.

28

You turn into a huge magnifying glass and begin to hunt for clues.

"WHAT ARE YOU DOING?" asks PAL. "THEY'RE GETTING AWAY!"

"I'm going to head to the vault and see what they've taken!"

"THAT'S CRAZY," says PAL. "FOLLOW THEM BEFORE THE TRAIL GOES COLD!"

To ignore PAL and head into the vault, go to 4.

To take PAL's advice, go to 11.

29

"The security systems won't spot a bird flying in," you say.

"GOOD IDEA!"

You turn into a blackbird and soon arrive at the Tower. You fly over the walls and land next to the Jewel Tower without being seen by any guards.

"I need to get inside," you tell PAL.

To turn into a creepy-crawly, go to 23.

To break in through a window, go to 45.

"The gang was seen heading into DIAMOND HQ, where the main diamond vault is located," says Crystal Gems. "You need to get here quickly!"

"Maybe I should turn into a rocket," you tell PAL. "I'd be there in seconds."

"NOT A GOOD IDEA," says PAL.

To turn into a rocket, go to 43.

To remain as a stealth jet, go to 12.

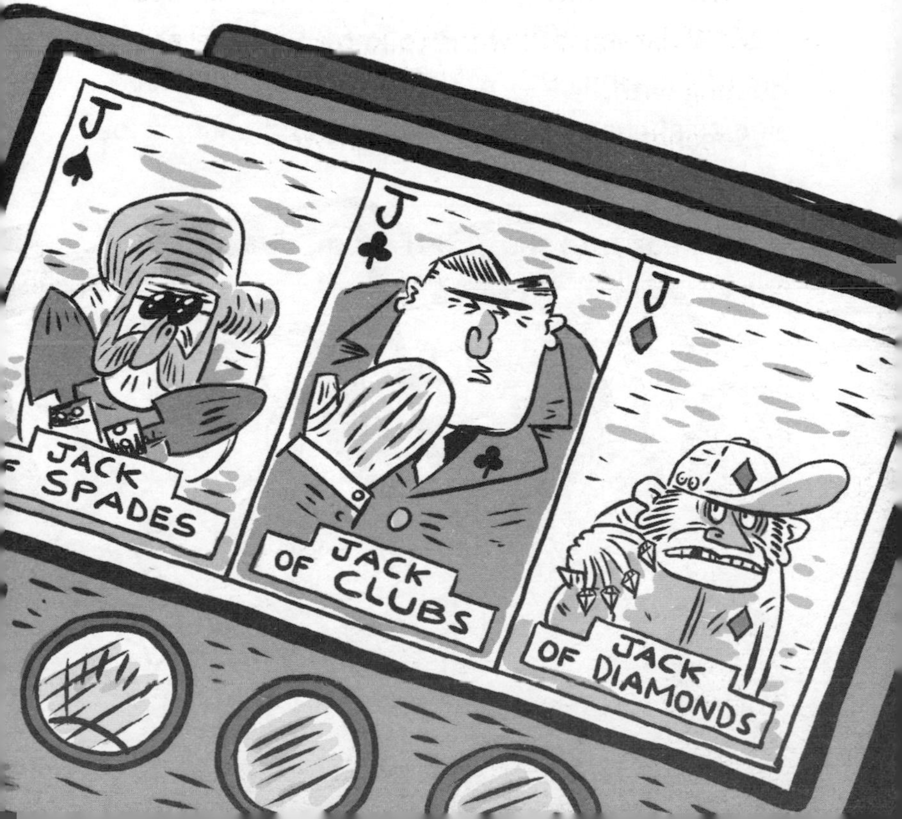
JACK SPADES
JACK OF CLUBS
JACK OF DIAMONDS

30

OK, turn me into a stealth jet," you tell PAL. "The gang won't see me coming!"

PAL obeys and soon you are an **F-35B** jet fighter, heading unseen towards Antwerp.

You open up a **COMMS** channel with Crystal Gems. "Can you tell me anything about the gang?" you ask.

"The leader is a woman and she's wearing a crown!"

"PAL, run that description through our ***MEGA VILLAIN*** database. I want to know who we are dealing with."

Seconds later PAL has the answer.

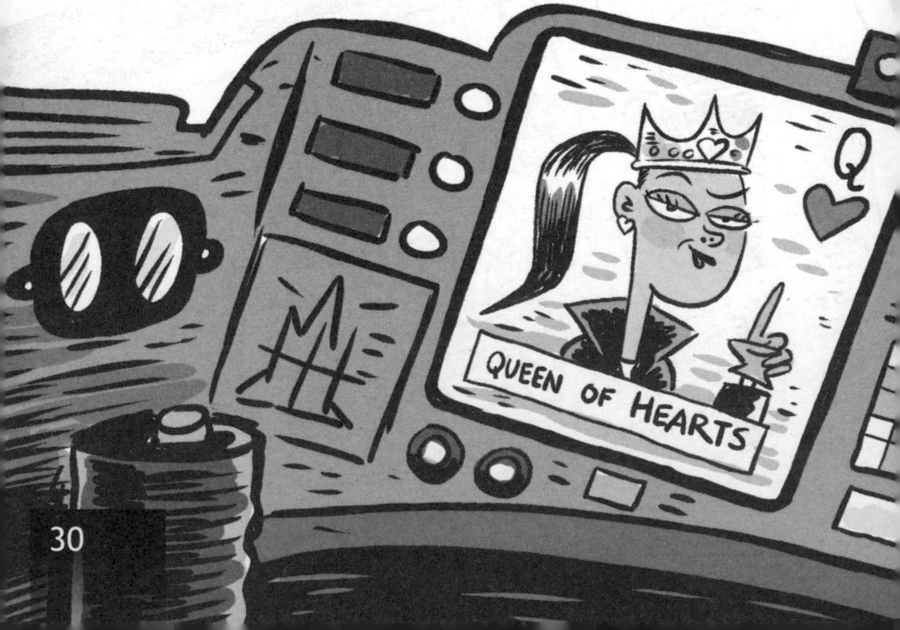
Q
QUEEN OF HEARTS

You turn into a battering ram and smash down the Jewel Tower's door. Inside is a hole in the floor.

That's how they got in, you think.

Suddenly the wall crumbles as **Spades** smashes through it and hurtles towards you, arms swinging.

Just before his deadly hands make contact, you transform into a **MEGA** voltage electrical cable.

ZAP!

The air crackles as **Spades**'s metal hands hit the cable. He is thrown backwards by the **MEGA** electrical charge and lies fizzing and unconscious on the ground.

To sneak into the jewel room, go to 47.
To charge in, go to 26.

32

The queen flicks through her playing cards. Seconds later she smiles. "The cards tell me that **MEGAHERO** is finally here!"

To try and capture the gang, go to 9.

To turn into human form, go to 14.

To attack the gang in wasp form, go to 22.

33

"PAL, turn me into a concrete block!"

The computer obeys and you transform. The tunnel stops collapsing as your concrete form secures the roof.

"I THINK YOU'VE MADE A BIT OF A BOO-BOO," says PAL.

"Why?" you reply. "I've stopped the tunnel collapsing."

"BUT WHAT HAPPENS WHEN YOU CHANGE FORM AGAIN? AT THAT MOMENT, IT'S GOING TO COLLAPSE ON TOP OF YOU, WHATEVER YOU TURN INTO. YOU'RE STUCK!"

DA-DA-DAAAH!

You blockhead! *Go back to 1.*

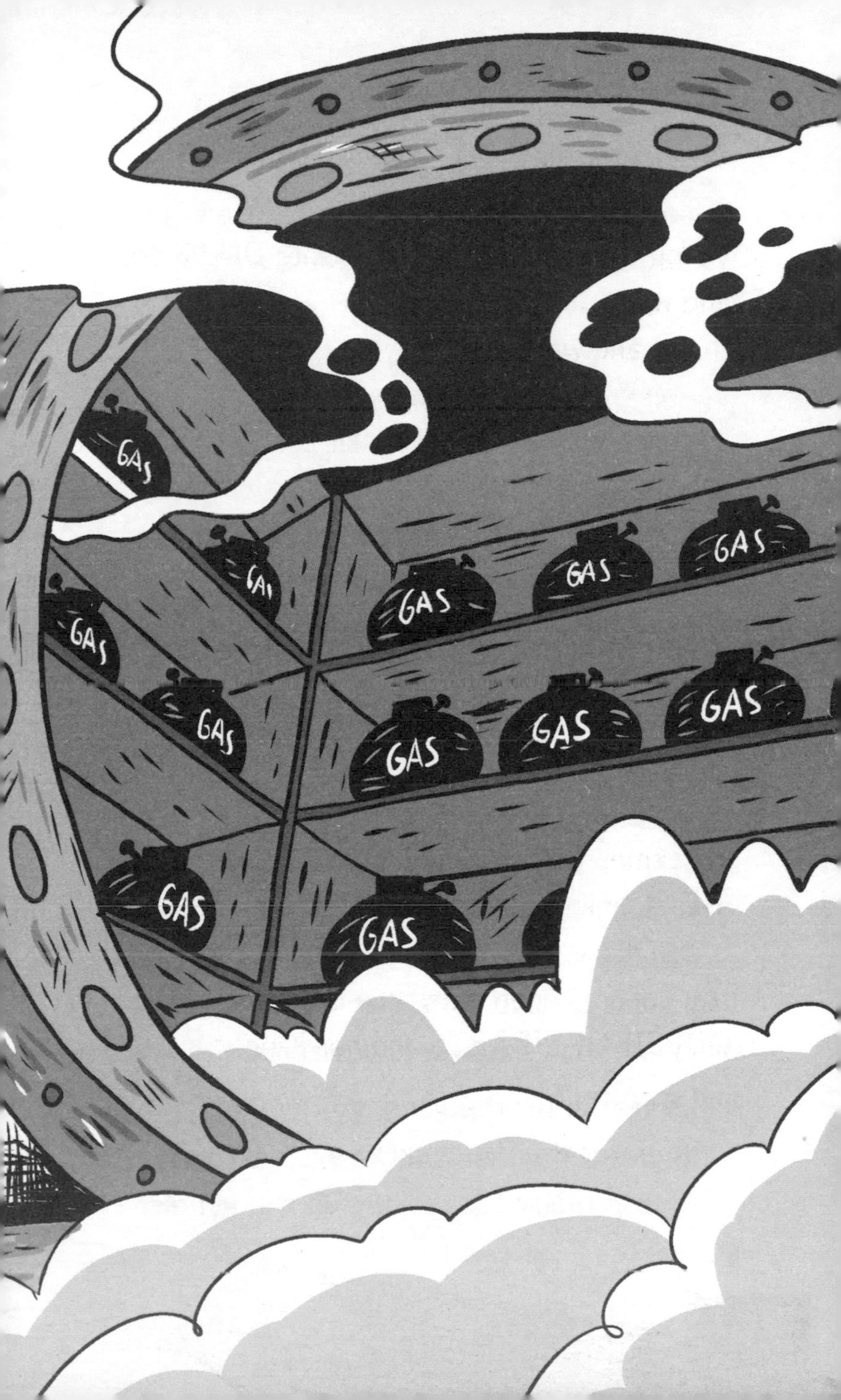
GAS
GAS
GAS
GAS
GAS
GAS
GAS
GAS
GAS
GAS
GAS
GAS

34

"OK," you say. "I'll wait with you."

You take up a position opposite DIAMOND HQ and wait ...

and wait ...

and wait ...

Eventually, PAL speaks. "ER, DON'T YOU THINK YOU SHOULD DO SOMETHING?"

"OK. I need to get in undetected. I'm in Antwerp, so turn me into an ant."

"YOU'RE MORE OF A TWERP," whispers PAL.

"I heard that!"

You transform into an ant and scurry into the building. You see several guards lying on the floor, unconscious.

"I smell gas," you tell PAL. "Maybe the gang used it to knock out the guards."

You make your way to the vault. The huge steel door is open but there is no sign of the QUEEN OF HEARTS and her gang.

To search for the gang, go to 20.

To enter the vault, go to 4.

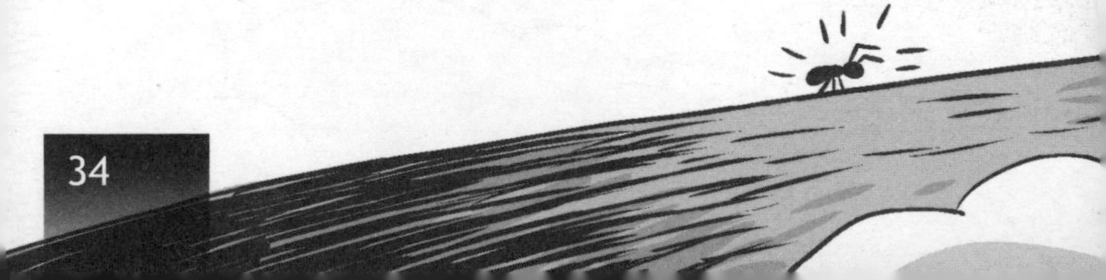

The queen smiles. "When I was a little girl I wanted to be like my sister, the **Queen of Diamonds**, with all her glittering jewels. Diamonds were her best friend. All I had were hearts! Squishy, lovey-dovey hearts!"

At that moment the glass cabinet shatters.

The queen gives a triumphant cry. "But now, I am going to have more diamonds and better diamonds than she ever had! Hand me the crown and sceptre!"

To give the queen the jewels, go to 41.

To stop Diamonds picking up the jewels, go to 17.

36

"Turn me into a giant paper shredder," you tell PAL.

You transform and shred the razor-sharp playing cards as they fly into your metal blades.

"That's the worst hand you've ever dealt," you say.

"I'll give you hands!" screams the queen. "Clubs, do your thing!"

The Jack of Clubs runs over to you, raising his huge, clubbed hands. Unable to move, you are helpless as he smashes your specs. He raises his hand ready to strike a final blow ...

DA-DA-DAAAH!

Your future has been shredded! *Go back to 1.*

Go back to 1.

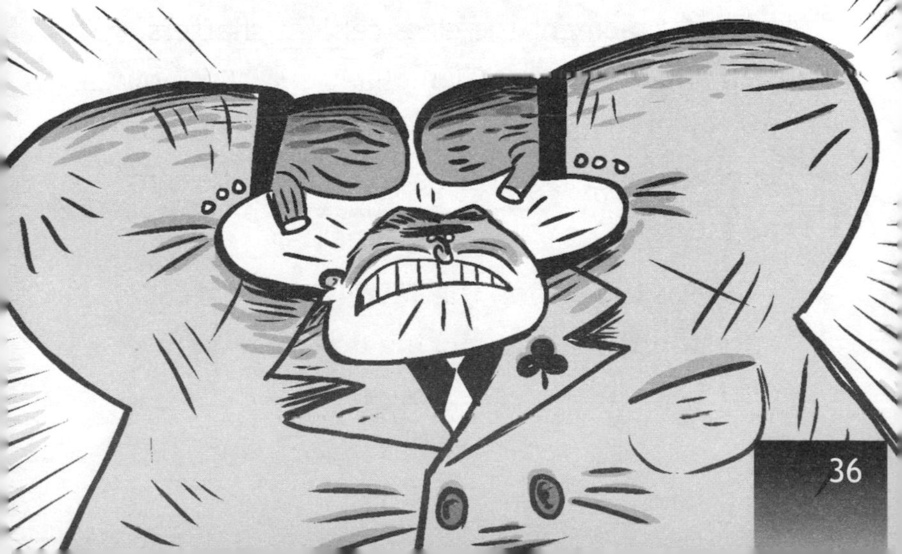

37

You transform into a scarecrow. The raven gives a frightened squawk and flies off.

But your change has attracted attention. A guard marches towards you.

"Now, why would a scarecrow be here?" he growls. "Maybe it's because it isn't really a scarecrow. Maybe it's ***MEGAHERO***!"

You see that the guard's hands are made of wood. It's the Jack of Clubs!

To attack Clubs, go to 21.

To talk to him, go to 2.

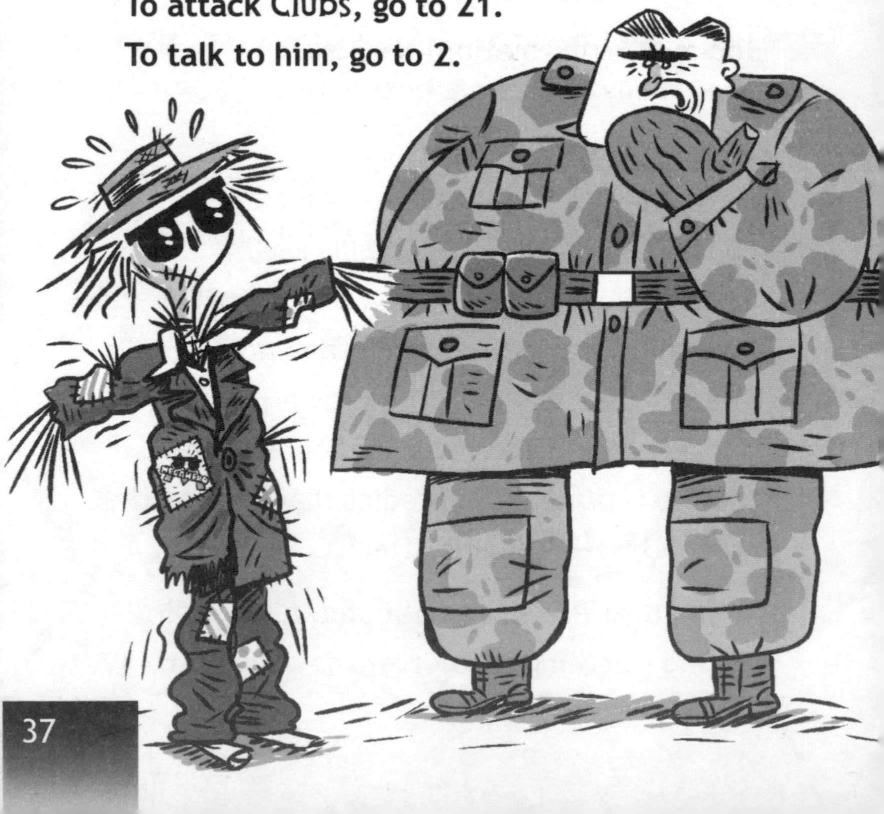

38

"Tell me more about the diamonds. Where are they held?" you ask.

"All over the city!" Crystal Gems gives you locations and PAL takes notes.

"Good. Now tell me about the gang," you say.

"This is taking too long!" moans the director. "Oh no! They're here, they're breaking down ..."

The screen goes blank.

"I think I need to get to Antwerp," you tell PAL.

"TOO LATE!" says PAL. "THE DIAMONDS HAVE GONE."

Too much information! **Go back to 1.**

39

"What do we know so far?" you ask.

"DIDN'T THE QUEEN SAY SOMETHING ABOUT COMMITTING THE BIGGEST DIAMOND ROBBERY EVER?"

"Yes, but what do you think that would be?"

"EASY," replies PAL. "The Crown jewels, which are kept in the Tower of London. The collection is priceless! I predict that is what the QUEEN OF HEARTS is after!"

To head to the Tower of London, go to 5.

To find out about the Crown jewels, go to 19.

40

You head downstairs. As you are in ant form, it takes some time to reach the ground floor.

You finally get to the diamond vault. The huge steel door is open but there is no sign of the gang.

To search for the gang, go to 20.
To enter the vault, go to 4.

41

You pick up the crown and sceptre. "I've fooled you. I'm not **Spades**, I'm **MEGAHERO**!" You transform.

"I knew that!" laughs the queen. "The cards foretold it! Now, give me the jewels!"

"If you insist!" You bop **Diamonds** on the head with the sceptre, knocking him out. "And now, I'm going to crown you!" Before the queen can react, you turn into a giant catapult and shoot the crown at her.

It hits her in the middle of her forehead and she drops to the floor, unconscious.

You turn back into human form.

"NOW THAT WAS A **GEM** OF A SHOT!" says PAL.

You laugh. "Yes, it seems that crime wasn't her best **suit**!"

Go to 50.

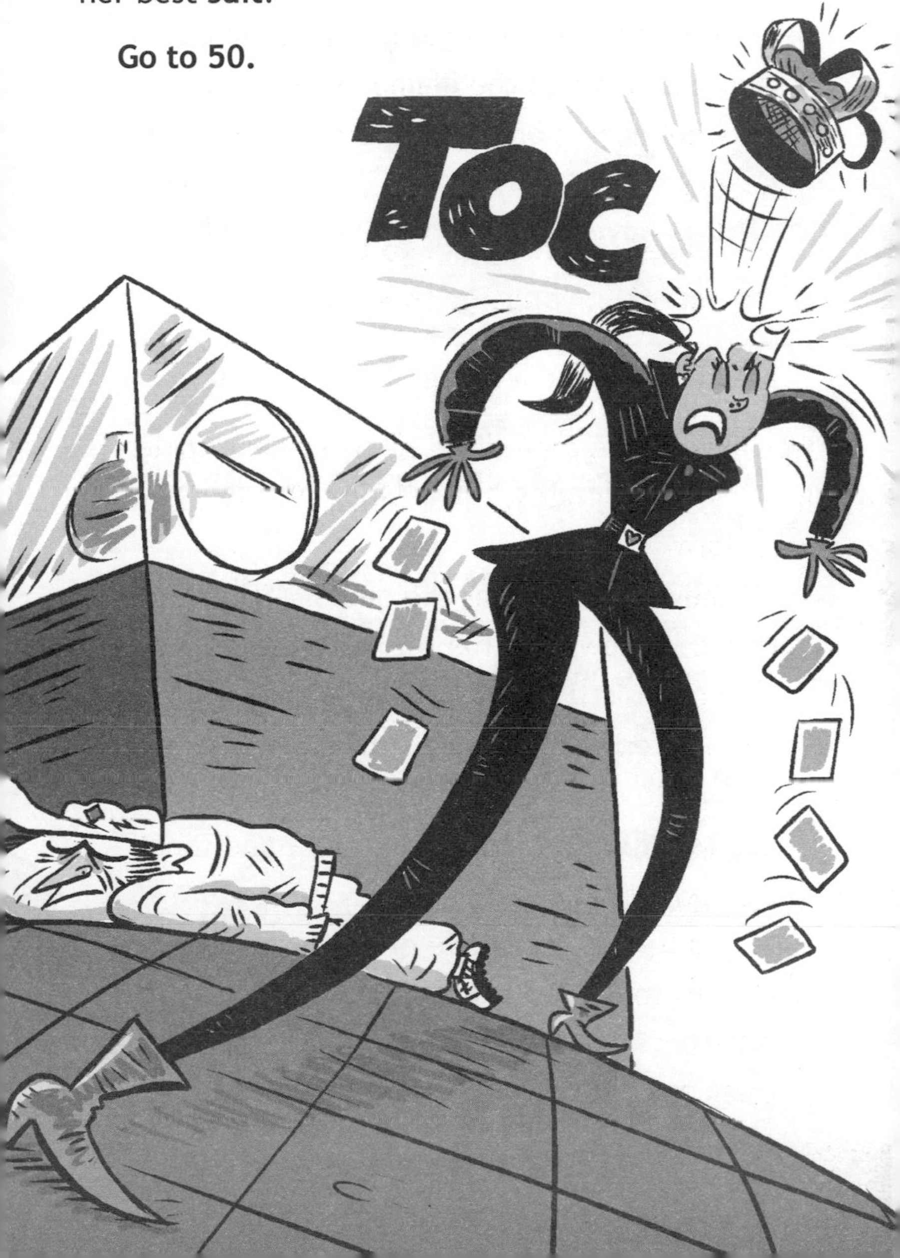
TOC

42

You run forward but the roof crashes down on you. You are trapped under hundreds of tons of rubble, unable to contact PAL ...

DA-DA-DAAAH!

Things have got on top of you! ***Go back to 1.***

43

"Just turn me into a rocket," you tell PAL.

"DON'T SAY I DIDN'T WARN YOU."

Seconds later you are zooming through the sky at ***MEGA*** speed.

You soon reach Antwerp. "OK, PAL, it's time to slow down. Turn me into a bird."

But you're going too fast! There's no time for PAL to change your form.

The ground gets nearer ...

DA-DA-DAAAH!

BOOM! PAL predicted that! ***Go back to 1.***

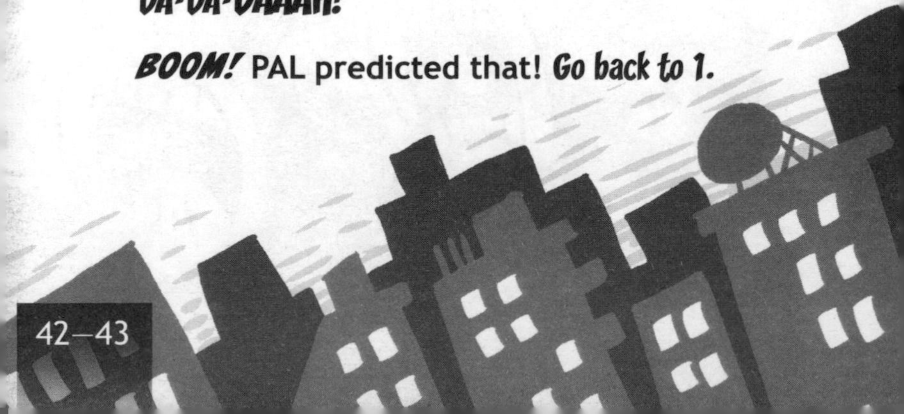

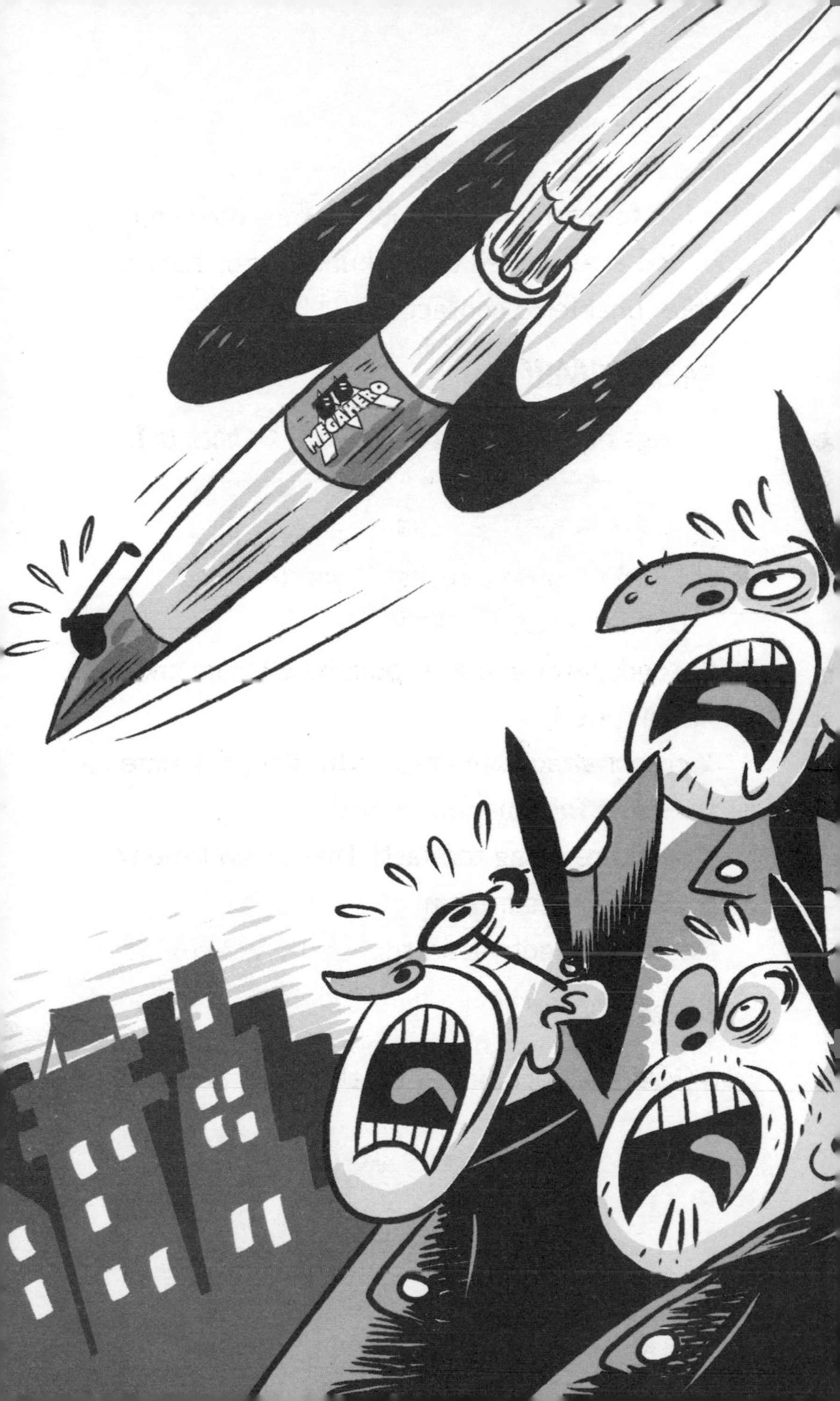
MEGAHERO

44

"Turn me into a giant pair of scissors," you say as the razor-sharp cards head towards you.

Suddenly you feel very warm and comfortable. "I said a pair of giant scissors, not giant slippers!

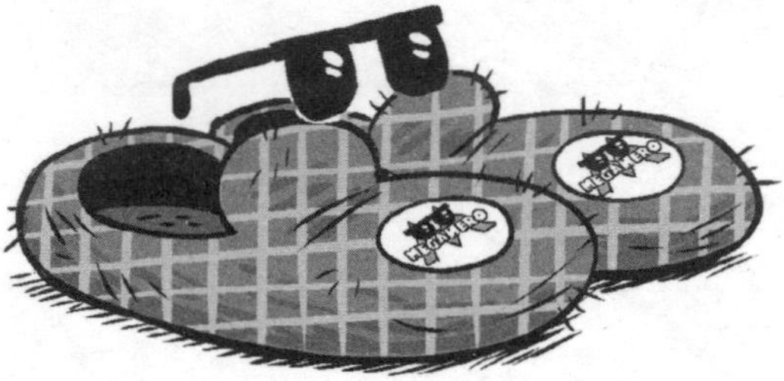
MEGAHERO
MEGAHERO

OW!" The cards hit you. "**QUICKLY!**"

"SORRY," says PAL, "I SLIPPED UP!"

Becoming scissors, you snip away at the cards and advance on the gang.

"Speed up, Spades!" orders the queen, unleashing another volley of cards.

The air is filled with cards, earth and clouds of dust. You are blinded by the debris. When the air clears, the gang has disappeared and there's a big hole in the floor!

To head down the hole straight away, go to 11.

To investigate the area first, go to 28.

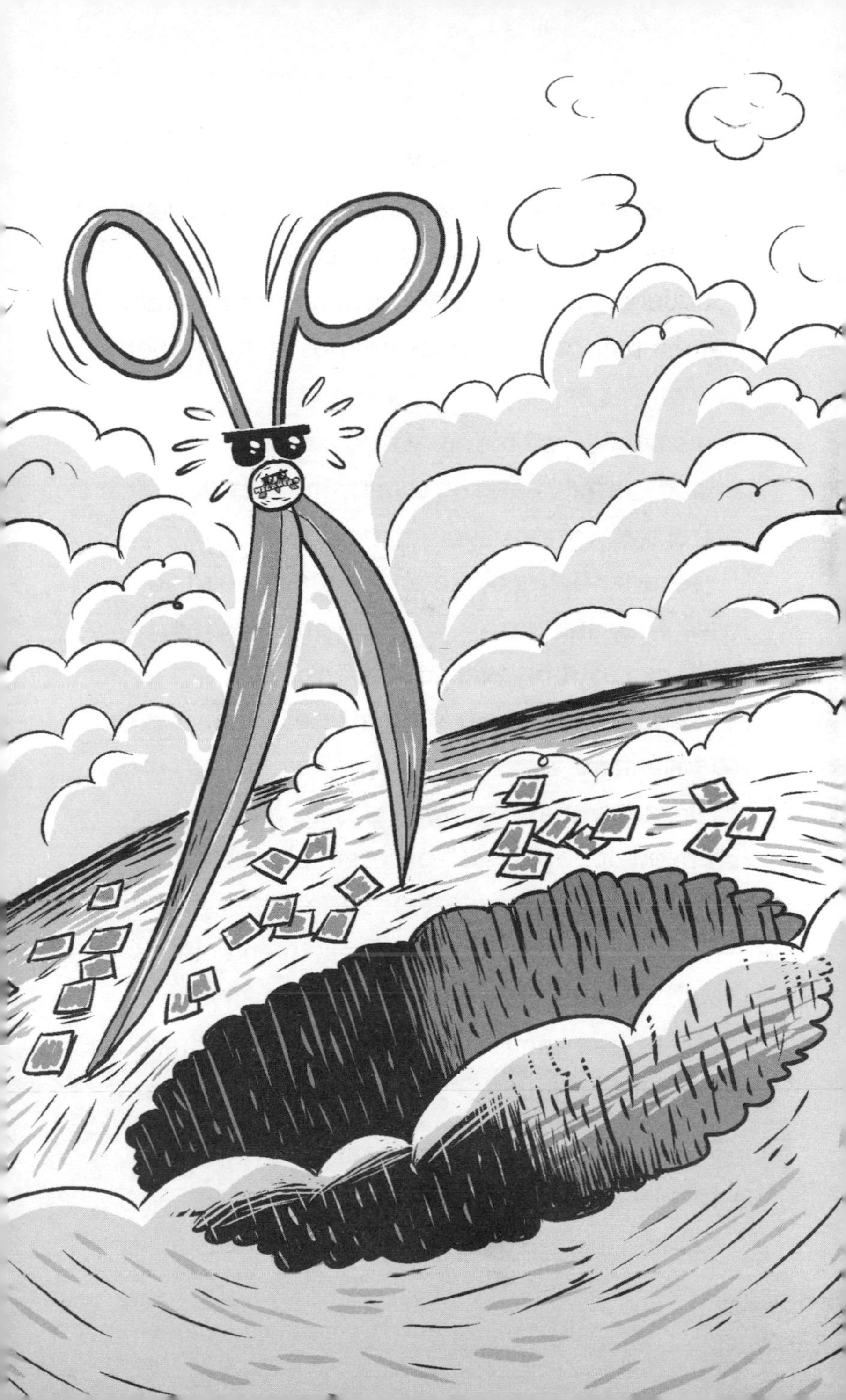

45

"Turn me into something that can get through this glass," you tell PAL.

Suddenly you are transformed into a giant hammer!

"THAT'LL BREAK GLASS," says PAL.

As nobody is holding you, you fall over with a loud crash. "I meant something that wouldn't attract attention!" you cry.

Security lights blaze and soldiers head your way. They stand over you, looking puzzled.

"I can explain everything," you say.

"A talking hammer with glasses. That is going to take some explaining."

A soldier snatches your glasses and stamps on them.

DA-DA-DAAAH!

Oh no, you've lost your PAL! ***Go back to 1.***

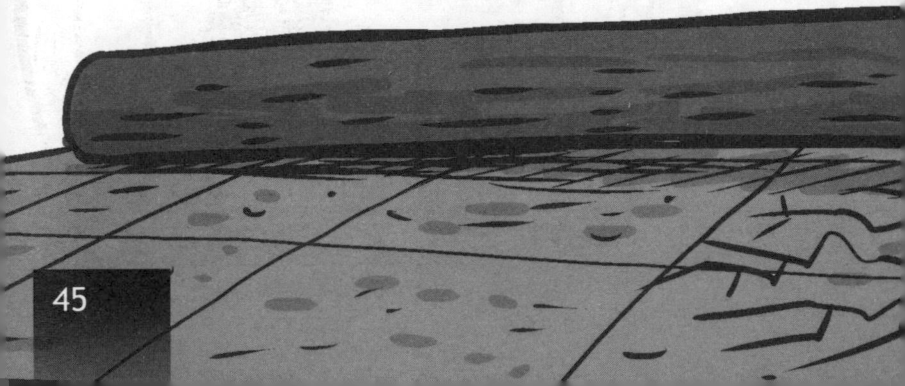

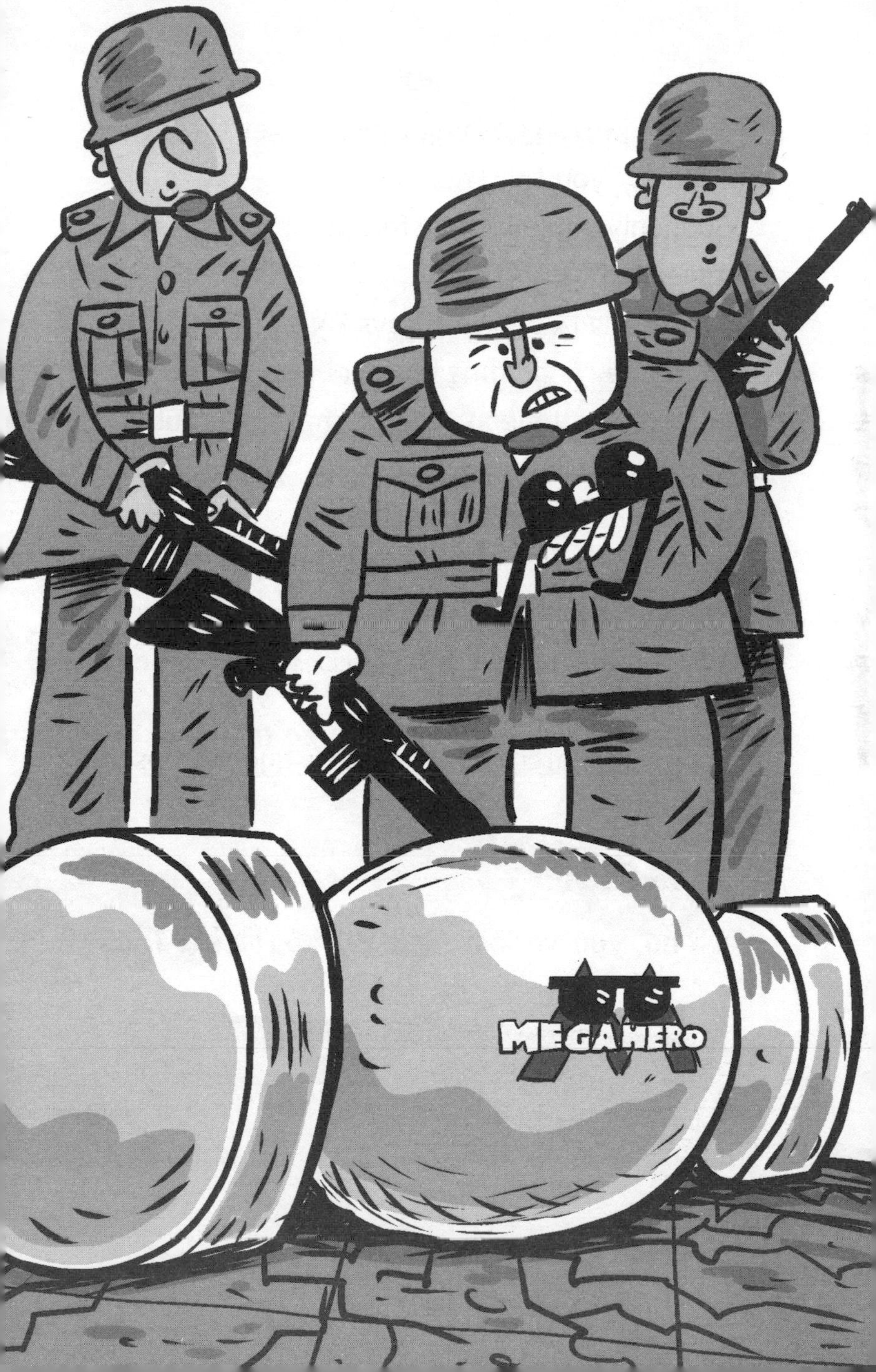
MEGAHERO

You buzz behind the gang as it makes its way from the vault with the diamonds.

The gang stops. "**Spades**, dig an escape tunnel," demands the queen.

You realise that the **Jack of Spades**'s hands are mechanical spades! He digs up the floor at amazing speed. Concrete and earth fly everywhere, hitting you smack in your waspy face!

"*OW!*" you cry.

The queen looks up. "Someone is here ..."

To remain in wasp form, go to 32.
To change into human form, go to 14.

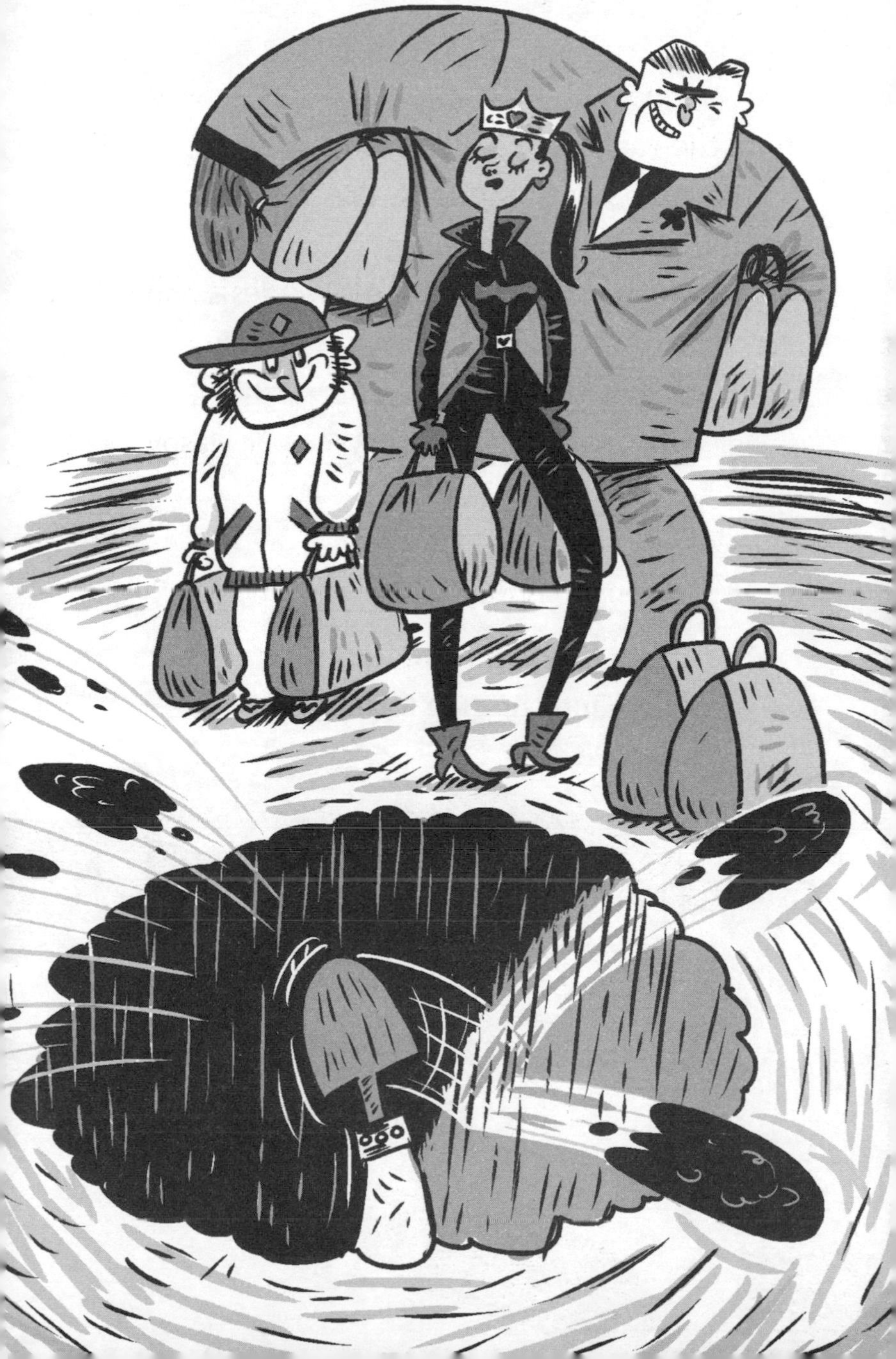

"Turn me into the Jack of Spades'" you tell PAL.

"NICE IDEA," replies the computer.

You transform and head into the jewel room. You see the Jack of Diamonds cutting into the glass case that holds the Crown jewels. The QUEEN OF HEARTS stands next to him.

"Did you deal with *MEGAHERO*?"

"Yes, Your Majesty."

"Good. Now get ready to grab the jewels when Diamonds gets through the glass!"

To stop Diamonds, go to 17.

To keep the queen talking, go to 35.

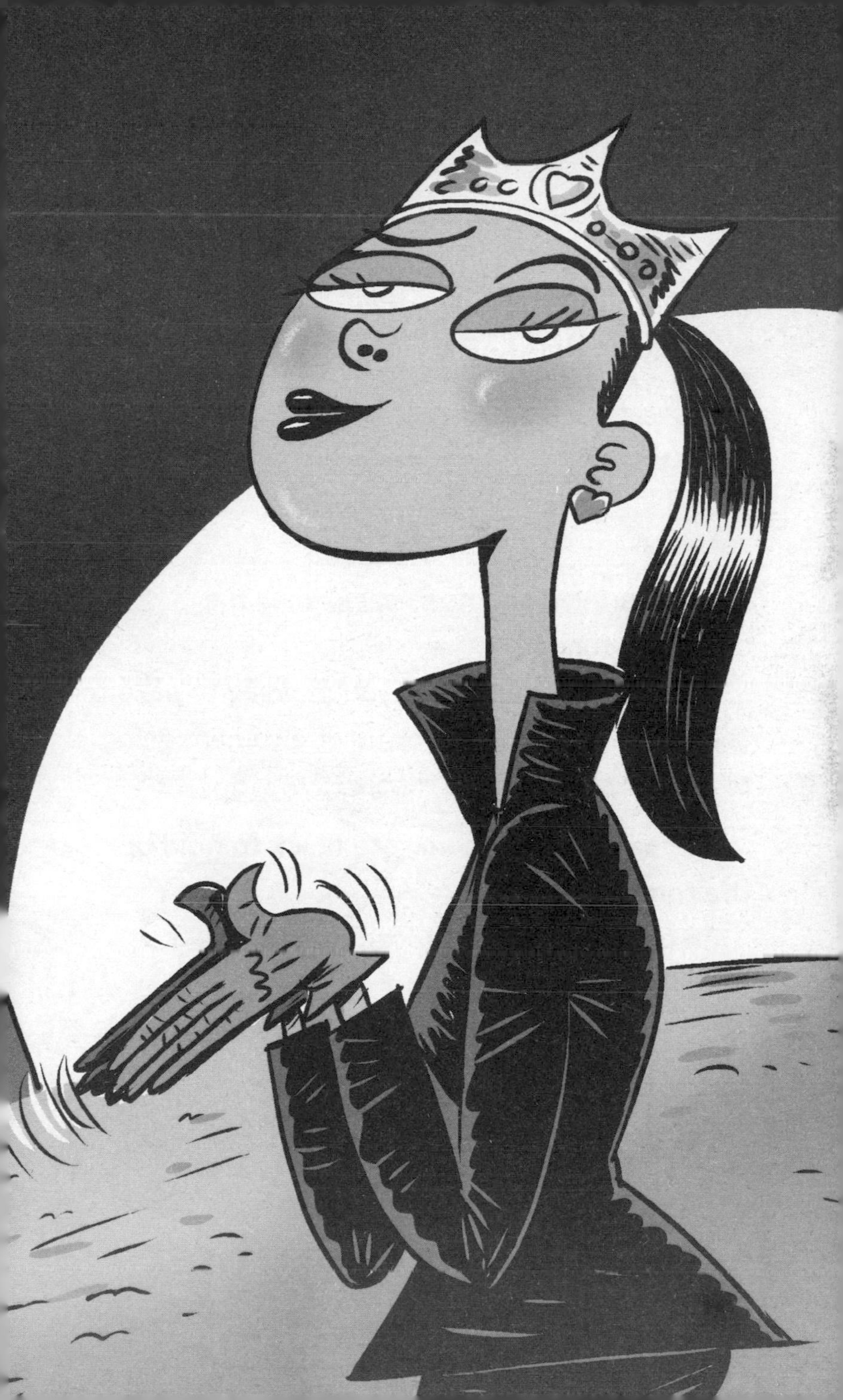

48

"OK, so let's carry on playing," you say.

"OF COURSE YOU NEED TO FIND OUT WHAT THE CRIME IS!" says PAL. "I WAS JOKING!"

"So was I," you smile. "You didn't predict that either!"

Go to 24.

49

You spin around and head back along the collapsing tunnel.

You quickly realise that you're going to have to change out of fox form, otherwise you are going to be buried under the rubble.

To change into a concrete block to hold up the tunnel, go to 33.

To change into a bulldozer, go to 15.

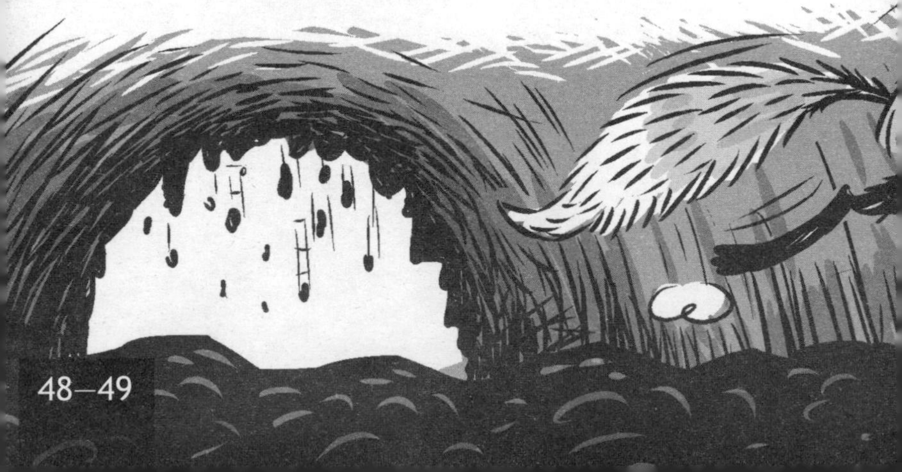

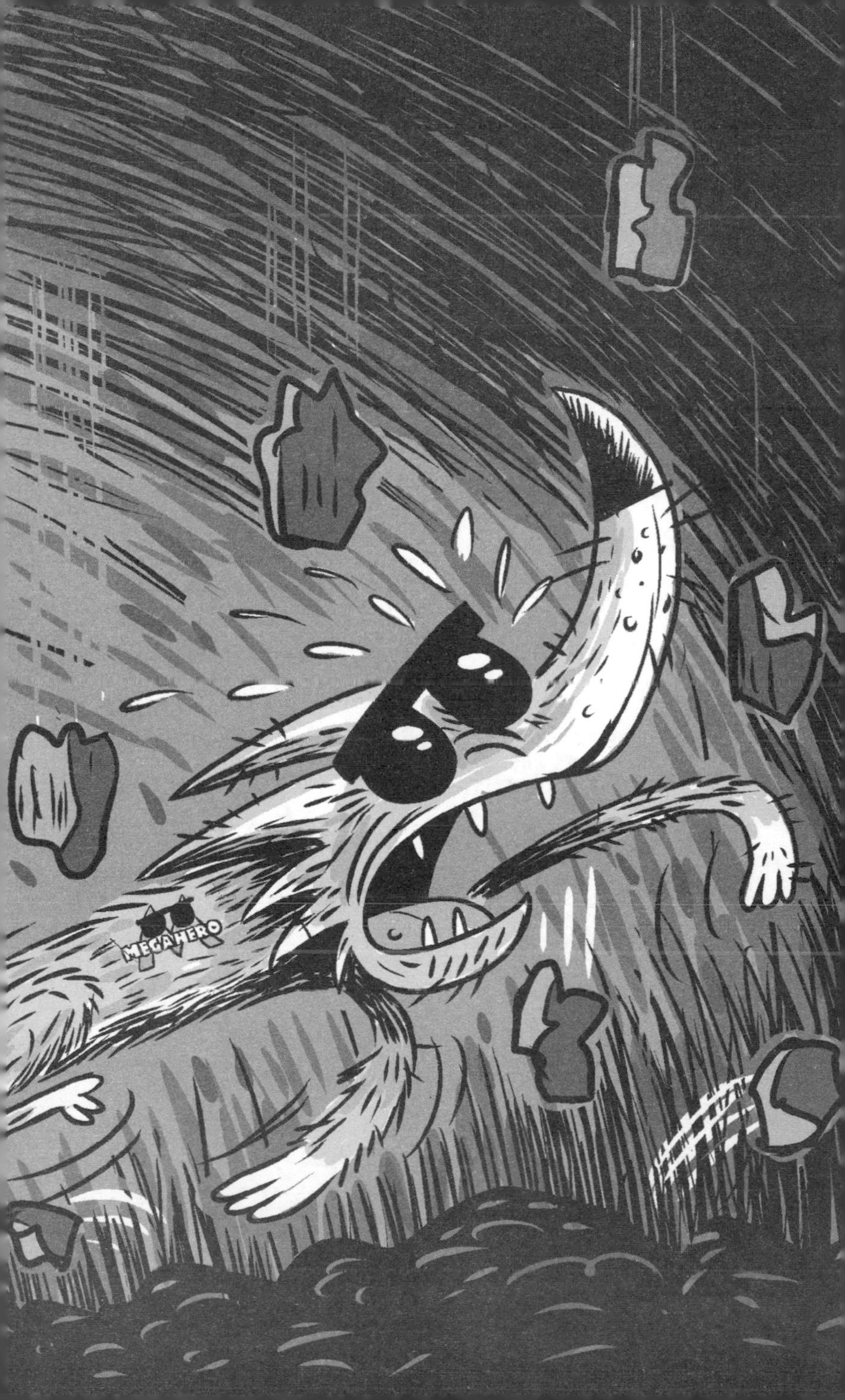
MEGAHERO

50

With the queen and her gang behind bars and the Crown jewels safely stored, you return to the ***MEGA*** cave.

"I predicted we'd trump the QUEEN OF HEARTS," says PAL. "HER DEFEAT WAS ALWAYS ON THE **CARDS**."

"We had all the tricks," you laugh. "She just couldn't **deal** with us!"

"NO," replies PAL. "SHE DIDN'T **PLAY HER CARDS** RIGHT."

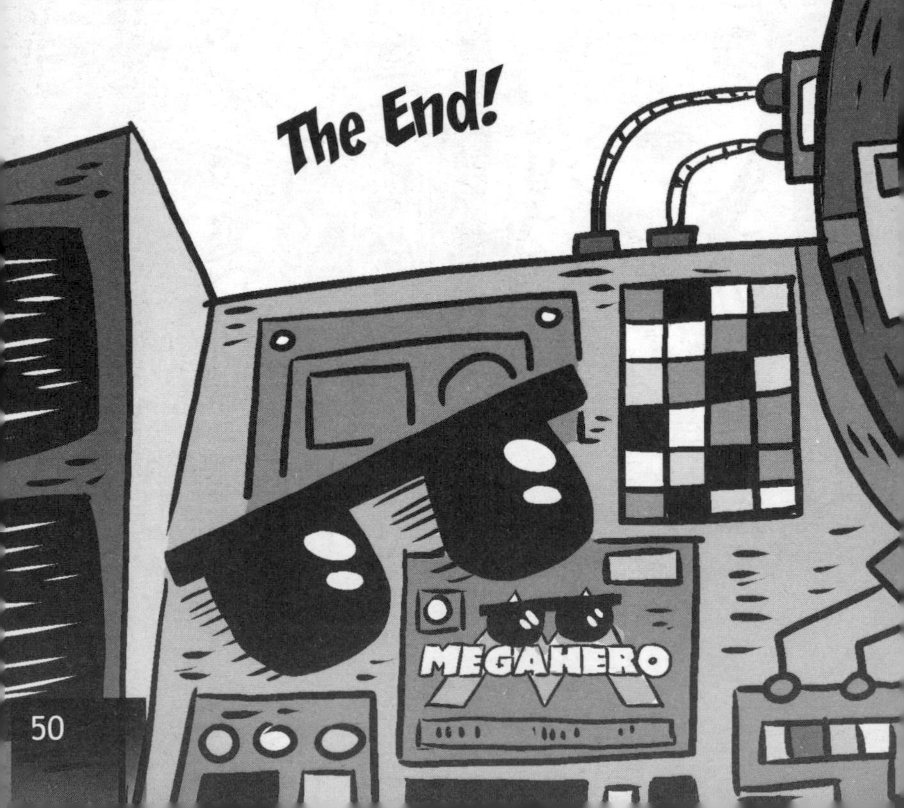
The End!
MEGAHERO

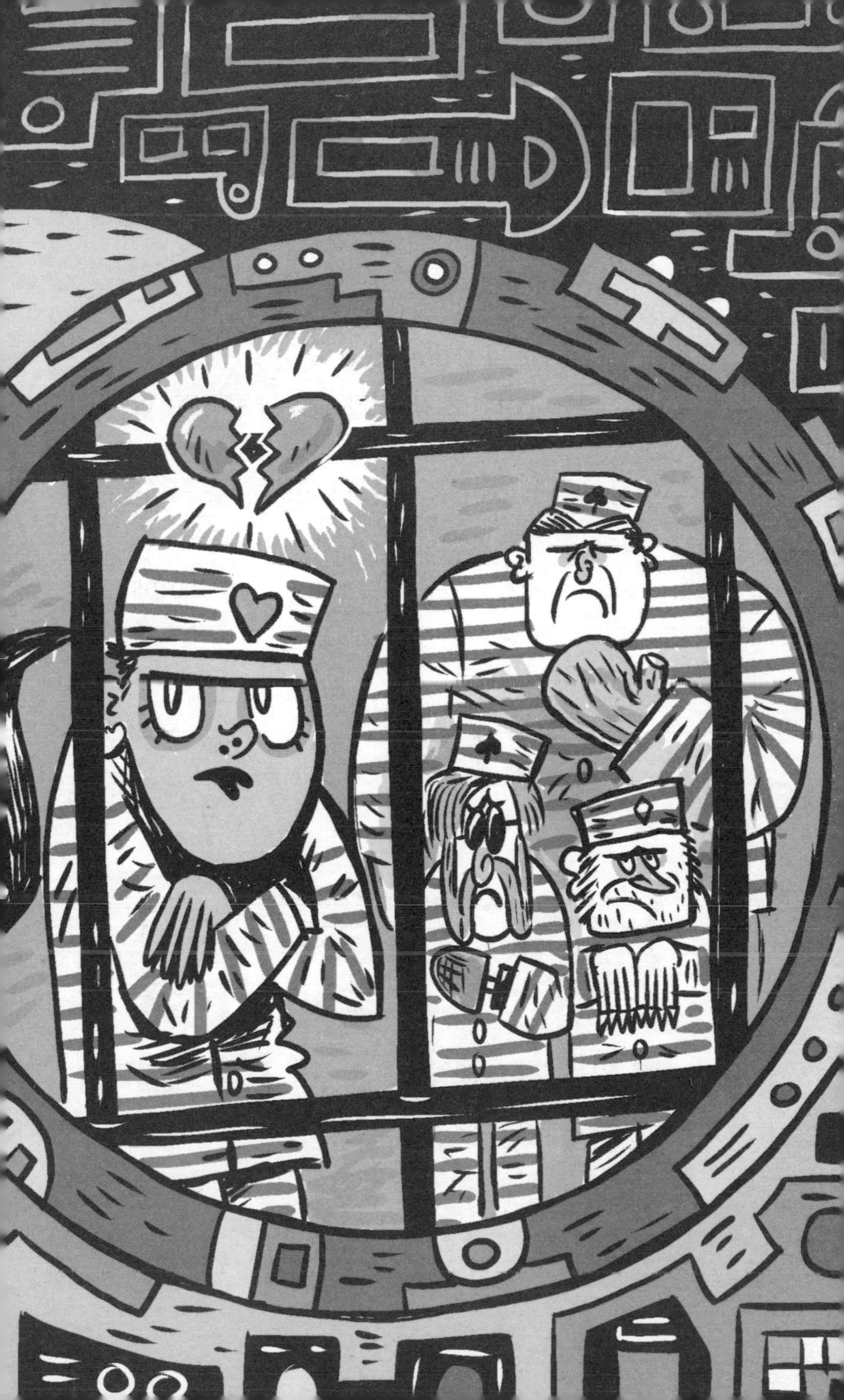

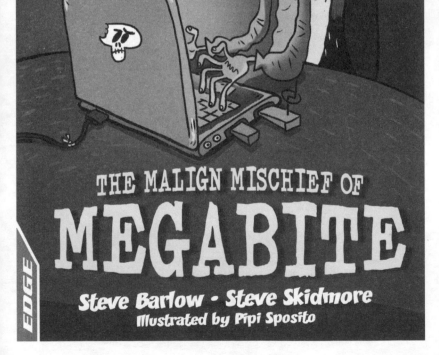

THE MALIGN MISCHIEF OF
MEGABITE

Steve Barlow · Steve Skidmore
Illustrated by Pipi Sposito

You are in the *MEGA* cave, surfing the Internet, looking for some new *MEGA* hero costume supplies on *PantsForMegaHeroes.net.*

"What about the blue underpants?" you ask PAL. "I'd look good in those!" You hit **BUY**.

"NOT REALLY YOUR COLOUR!" says PAL. "HOW ABOUT BROWN, THEN IT WON'T SHOW ANY ... **WHAAARGHHHHHH! FIZZ! FLIPPITY FIZZ! BUZZ, ZOINK!**"

The *MEGA* cave lights up as PAL's circuits begin fizzing and popping!

"What's the matter?" you ask.

"SECURITY SYSTEMS BREACHED," gasps PAL. "SOMETHING'S GOT INTO MY SYSTEM!"

"But that's impossible," you say. "You have *MEGA* firewalls! Nothing should be able to get through them!"

Flames and smoke begin to shoot out of PAL's circuits. "I THINK THAT MIGHT BE A WRONG ASSUMPTION! **HELP!**"

To reboot PAL, go to 14.

To try and put the fire out, go to 38.

CONTINUE THE ADVENTURE IN:

THE MALIGN MISCHIEF OF

MEGABITE

About the 2Steves

"The 2Steves" are
Britain's most popular
writing double act for
young people, specialising
in comedy and adventure.
They perform regularly in
schools and libraries, and at festivals, taking the
power of words and story to audiences of all ages.

Together they have written many books, including the
I HERO Immortals and *I HERO Toons* series.

About the illustrator:
Pipi Sposito

Pipi was born in Buenos Aires in
the fabulous 60's and has always
drawn. As a little child, he used
to make modelling clay figures, too.
At the age of 19 he found out
he could earn a living by drawing. He now develops
cartoons and children's illustrations in different
artistic styles, and also 3D figures, puppets and
caricatures. Pipi always listens to music when he works.

Have you completed these I HERO adventures?

I HERO Immortals — more to enjoy!

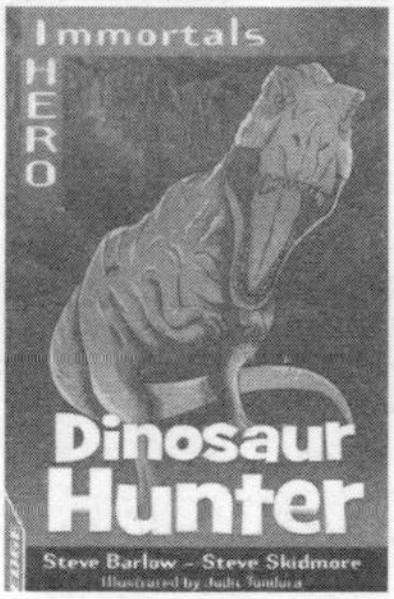
Immortals
HERO
Dinosaur Hunter
Steve Barlow – Steve Skidmore

978 1 4451 6963 7 pb
978 1 4451 6964 4 ebook

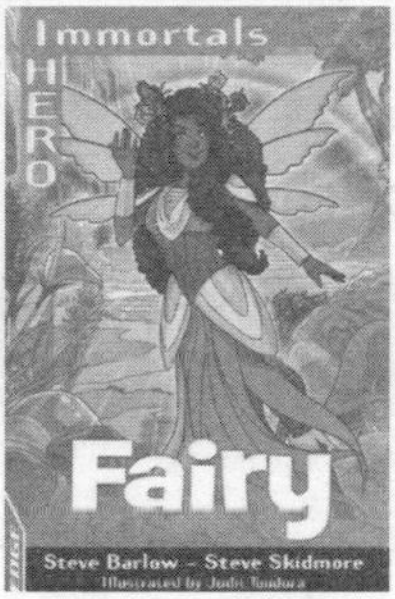
Immortals
HERO
Fairy
Steve Barlow – Steve Skidmore

978 1 4451 6969 9 pb
978 1 4451 6971 2 ebook

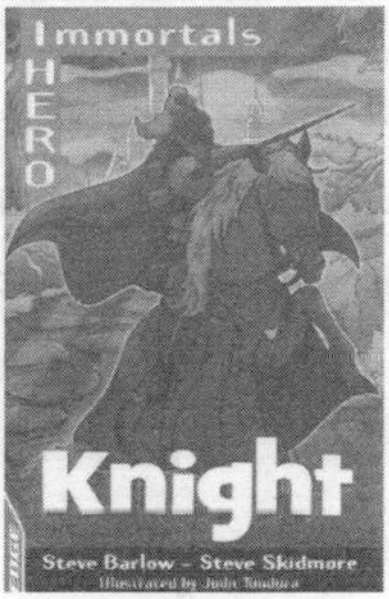
Immortals
HERO
Knight
Steve Barlow – Steve Skidmore

978 1 4451 6957 6 pb
978 1 4451 6959 0 ebook

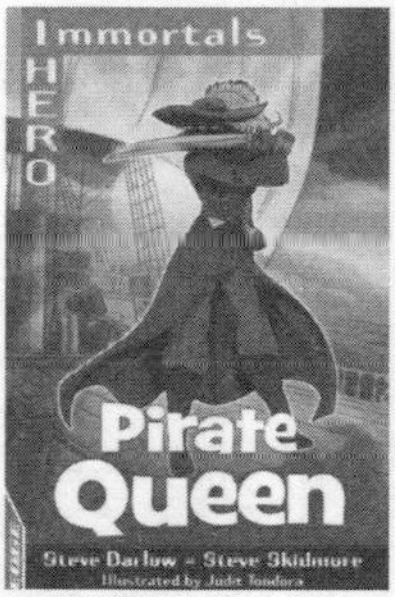
Immortals
HERO
Pirate Queen
Steve Barlow – Steve Skidmore

978 1 4451 6954 5 pb
978 1 4451 6955 2 ebook

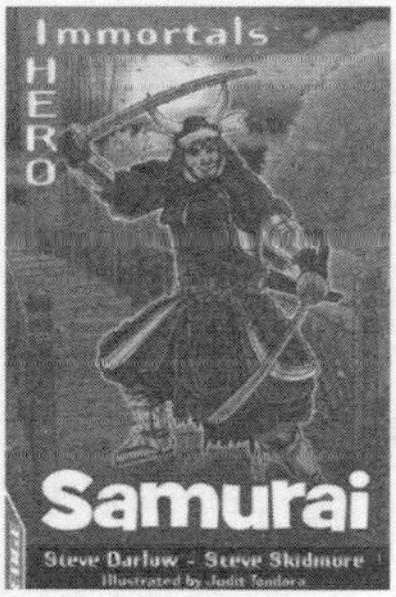
Immortals
HERO
Samurai
Steve Barlow – Steve Skidmore

978 1 4451 6960 6 pb
978 1 4451 6962 0 ebook

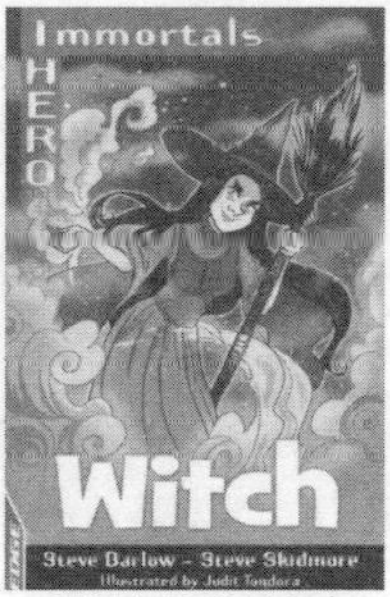
Immortals
HERO
Witch
Steve Barlow – Steve Skidmore

978 1 4451 6966 8 pb
978 1 4451 6967 5 ebook

Defeat all the baddies in Toons:

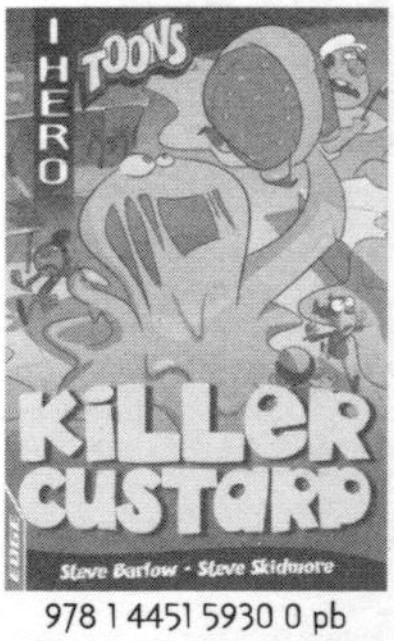
I HERO
TOONS
Killer Custard
Steve Barlow - Steve Skidmore

978 1 4451 5930 0 pb
978 1 4451 5931 7 ebook

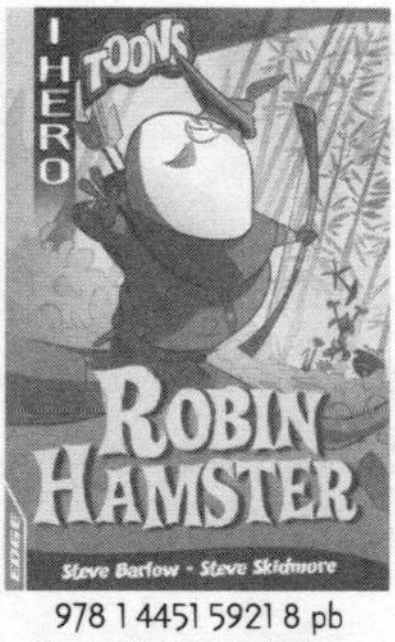
I HERO
TOONS
Robin Hamster
Steve Barlow - Steve Skidmore

978 1 4451 5921 8 pb
978 1 4451 5922 5 ebook

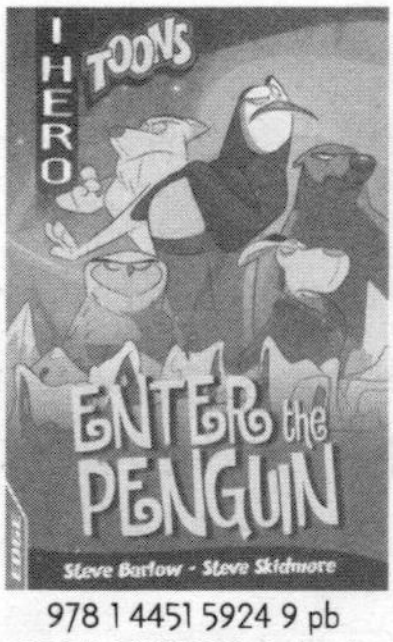
I HERO
TOONS
Enter the Penguin
Steve Barlow - Steve Skidmore

978 1 4451 5924 9 pb
978 1 4451 5925 6 ebook

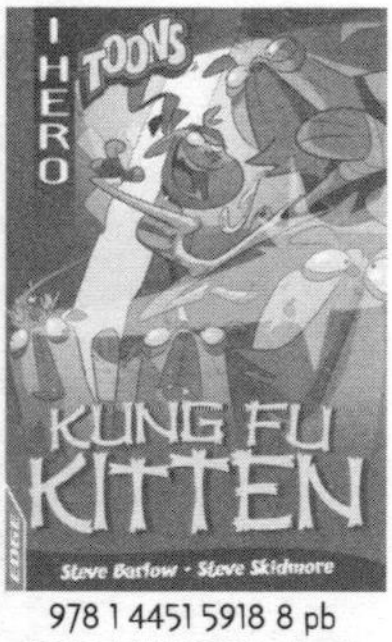
I HERO
TOONS
Kung Fu Kitten
Steve Barlow - Steve Skidmore

978 1 4451 5918 8 pb
978 1 4451 5919 5 ebook

Also by the 2Steves...

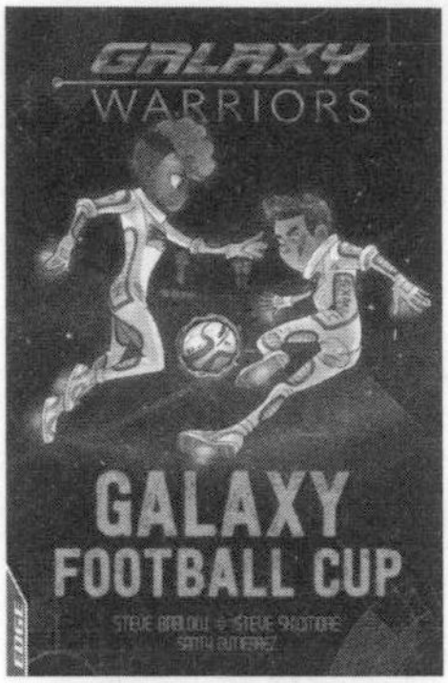
GALAXY
WARRIORS
GALAXY
FOOTBALL CUP

978 1 4451 5985 0 hb
978 1 4451 5986 7 pb

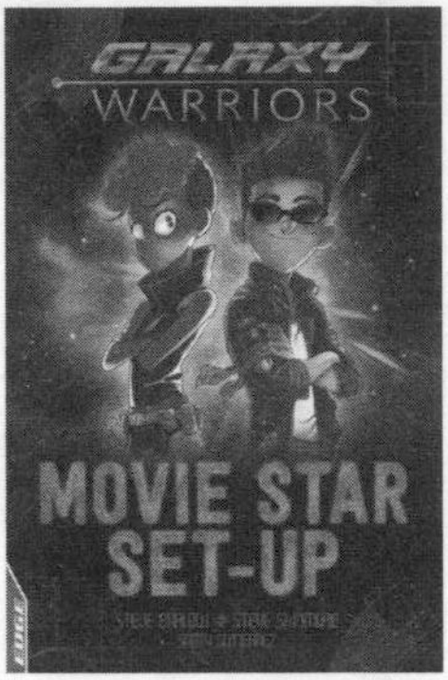
GALAXY
WARRIORS
MOVIE STAR
SET-UP

978 1 4451 5976 8 hb
978 14451 5977 5 pb

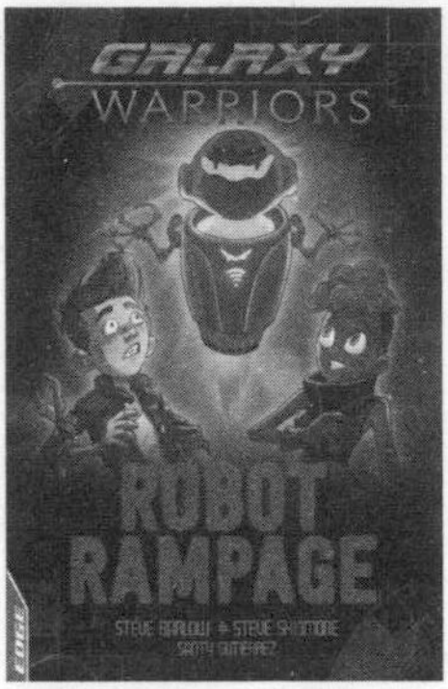
GALAXY
WARRIORS
ROBOT
RAMPAGE

978 1 4451 5982 9 hb
978 1 4451 5983 6 pb

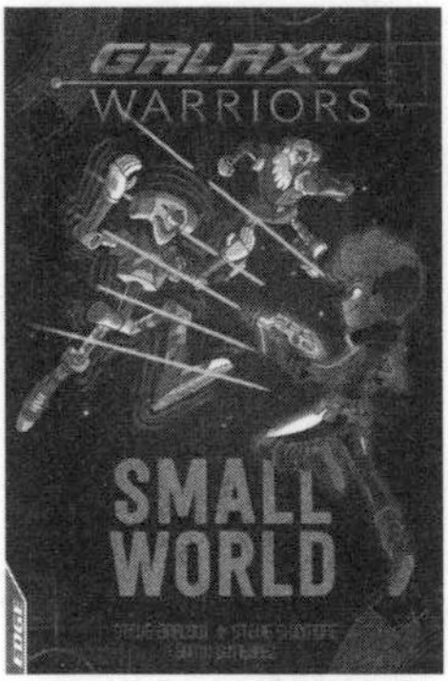
GALAXY
WARRIORS
SMALL
WORLD

978 1 4451 5972 0 hb
978 1 4451 5971 3 pb

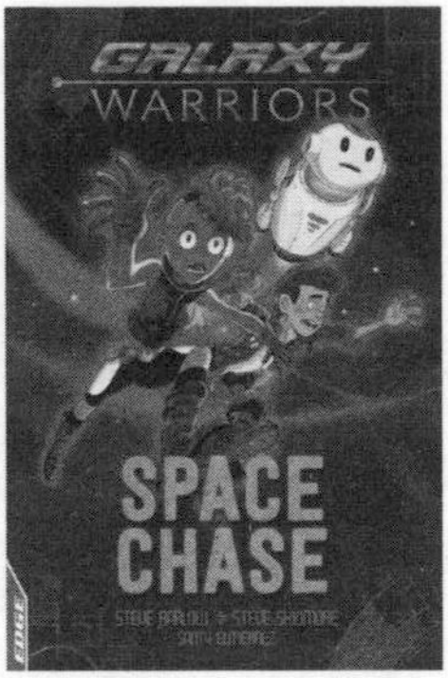
GALAXY
WARRIORS
SPACE
CHASE

978 1 4451 5892 1 hb
978 1 4451 5891 4 pb

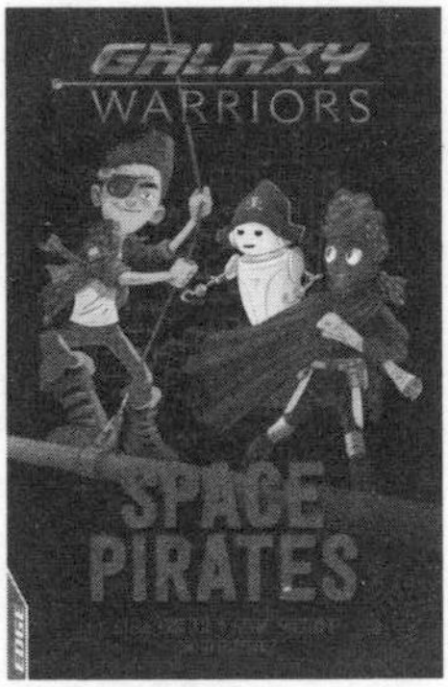
GALAXY
WARRIORS
SPACE
PIRATES

978 1 4451 5988 1 hb
9781 4451 5989 8 pb

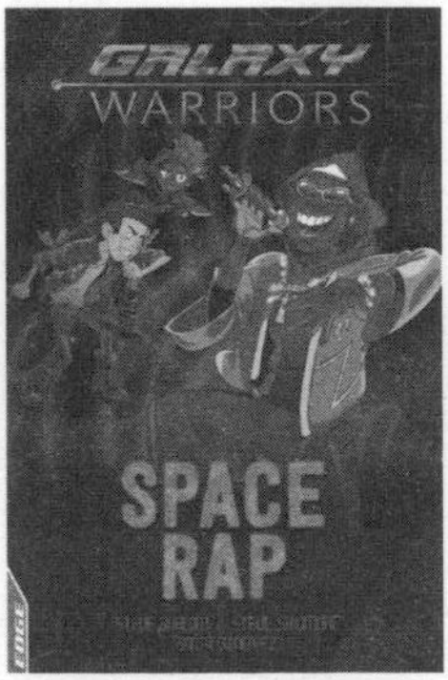
GALAXY
WARRIORS
SPACE
RAP

978 1 4451 5973 7 hb
978 1 4451 5974 4 pb

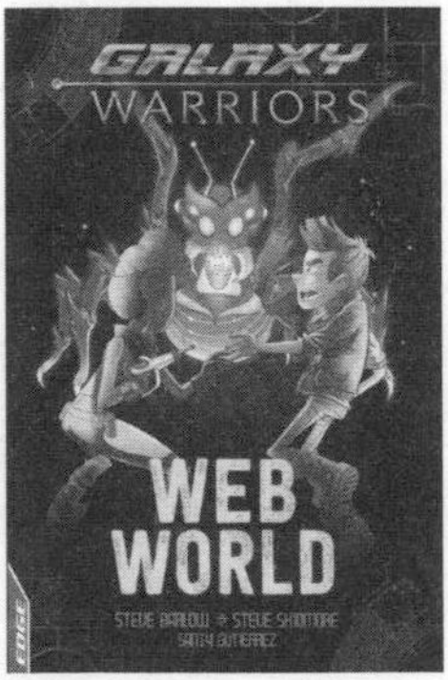
GALAXY
WARRIORS
WEB
WORLD

978 1 4451 5979 9 hb
978 1 4451 5980 5 pb